Some Horrific Evening

Mary E. Hart

Mary E Hart

Hart

ISBN: 978-1-547-13295-9 (paperback)
ISBN: 1-547-13295-7 (e-book)

DEDICATION

This, my first book, is for the little dude who will always be my little dude, even though he's now taller than I am. Your imagination and sense of humor inspires me daily, Adam. Thanks for keeping me motivated by continuing to ask me when my book was going to be finished and published.

ACKNOWLEDGMENTS

First, thanks to my subconscious for the dream that sparked this book idea in the first place.

Thank you to my parents, Dave & Maureen, for instilling such a strong love of reading all types of books in me and giving me the confidence to never give up on my dreams. You mean the world to me.

To my husband, Scott, and our son, Adam, thank you both for dealing with me working on this book all the time. Little dude, this one's for you!

To Lisa, thank you for your friendship throughout all of these years, and for being the first one besides me to read this in its entirety.

To my friends who read this in various iterations (including when it was pure crap in the very early stages) and always inspire me and keep me going, thank you!

PROLOGUE

"Why is this house trying to keep me locked in here? Let me out! I don't belong here!"

Great. Now I have Radiohead's song, "Creep" (or "Creek" as we called it back in school – queen of misheard lyrics here, folks. When I sing it, the lyrics are "I'm a creek. I'm a river…") stuck in my head.

Stop it! That's not helping… Okay, I need to concentrate. Come on. Think. I need to find a way out to get help. Can that window open?

Nope. Of course it doesn't. That would be too easy. Grrr...

"Dammit! Let me out of here! I don't want to die!"

CHAPTER 1

24 Hours Earlier...

"You lucky little bitch!," Kitty Malloy squealed, throwing herself at me for a hug as I rushed into the Ellerbee Events office on Newbury Street in Boston that morning, almost stumbling over my own feet whilst carrying my usual large hot White Chocolate Mocha latte to fend off the winter's chill.

"Or do I need to start calling you Miss Hartwell," Kitty continued, "seeing as how you're now the big fancy Event Producer for our largest local event of the year??!! Why didn't you tell me you're leading the planning for the Winter Dance, Maura?!? I had to find out when I got the request for the final go-over at the mansion. I'm so jealous I could die."

"Oh, you know Ashley would be handling it herself if she wasn't going to be out of the country ensuring the latest Kardashian wedding goes off without a hitch," I said, extricating myself gently from Kitty's hug so I could set down my drink without spilling it and hang my long black pea coat up on the coat rack next to my desk. "I'm sure she just chose me instead of you or Travis only because I've been working for her the longest and no other reason."

I was flushing quite a bit and hoping that the Ashley in question -- Ashley Ellerbee, the owner of Ellerbee Events and our boss -- wasn't hearing this and re-thinking putting her trust in me to make this event happen.

"Stop selling yourself short," said Kitty. "You always do that! You're smart and creative and have a great eye. This is going to be a fantastic event and if not, well…" she continued with a teasing twinkle in her eye, "Ashley will just fire you. No big, right?"

Oh, lord. No pressure at all. Nope. None. Do you think if I keep repeating that to myself, it'll make it so?

Hell, I've been working for Ashley for close to a decade, since about a year after I graduated from college. In that time, I've learned so much about events through Ashley and some classes I took on my own, so some of that knowledge and wisdom must have stuck. At least I hope it did.

I started out at Ellerbee Events as an Event Assistant getting coffee, answering phones, setting appointments and making dry cleaner runs — all the usual assistant grunt work -- but at the same time I also learned from Ashley about what goes into a great event and all the little details that make it happen. Over the past years, I worked my way up to being an Event Planner, and I love it.

There's just one downside to the job. Working all these nights and weekends hasn't left me much time (okay, no time whatsoever) for a social life minus the occasional date; hanging out with my coworker friends; and catching up with others through Facebook posts, messages and texts, but that is what it is. Ashley, on the other hand, has managed to keep her business thriving while also having a social life. Heck, she even got engaged three years ago to Ryan Alder, a construction worker who helps us out with events by building whatever we need, from backdrops to chuppahs, and his team also sets up the lighting for us.

Ashley and Ryan just look perfect together -- she looks like a real-life Barbie with a trim figure and insanely long legs to die for along with long, shiny, straight blonde hair and sparkling blue eyes. Ryan complements her well as he's a very tall, rugged version of Ken with brown eyes; dark brown hair that's close-cropped on the side and back with a permanently mussed, jagged section on the top; a solid jawline; and strong, muscular arms.

Oh, those arms… How could a girl miss them when he's working for us and has his sleeves rolled up? Or when it gets hot and he removes his denim shirt and is sporting a tank top with his skin glistening in the heat? Or, hell, when it's just so hot that the tank top comes off revealing his sweaty pecs as just the two of us are working in a room on a hot, sultry weekend and I reach over on impulse to follow the trail of one of the droplets of sweat down his broad chest and taut abs with my finger as Ryan pulls me to him...

Woah. Caught myself in a bit of an embarrassing daydream there, which is happening a bit too often. Down, girl. Yes, it doesn't hurt to look and all that, of course, but that's your boss' fiancé you're perving over. He's taken, so he's off limits. Enough said. Plus, Ashley would kick your ass if she found out about it, after laughing at you. Knock it off! Hmm, maybe I should have chosen an iced drink over a hot one, since I now needed to cool off.

Hopefully I'll get over these ridiculous fantasies when they finally get married, whenever that may be. Their wedding date is the big question since they've been engaged so long and have yet to set a date. These days, though, they're hardly spending any time hitting the town together that I can see. Ashley's been spending more nights working on this celebrity wedding than out with Ryan, so their own wedding planning is probably just being put on hold until after this one's over.

In fact, Ryan has actually spent more time with me, Kitty, and our other coworker, Travis, over the past six months on our outings to play pool, go bowling, or just grab some drinks after work than he has with Ashley. If Ashley wasn't so busy with all the planning she's doing for the Kardashian wedding, I'd think it was odd, but I know she's been swamped making sure everything is in order.

Ryan did always seem to have a fun time when he was out with us, since I'm sure he'd figure out an excuse to not join if he wasn't enjoying himself. But I had to admit that for the most part, him being there always made me more tense and quiet than I'd usually be when out with my friends.

Yes, there were a number of times when I was having so much fun that I forgot to have my guard up and actually cracked a joke around him, talked instead of hiding in the corner, or was my usually silly self, and Ryan would always look a bit surprised by that, which makes sense considering how subdued I was otherwise.

However, I usually kept my demeanor almost business-like in order to not let my stupid little crush on him show at all since I didn't want to come across like a spaz or, heaven forbid, let my feelings show even remotely. It would have been easier if Ashley was able to make it to hang out, since she's a solid reminder that he's taken, but she's been too busy the past year to make it to an outing.

Part of me actually wishes that Ashley wasn't going to be out of the country working on that wedding during the Winter Dance so that she could be the one managing it and it wouldn't fall on me. However, weddings like the Kardashian one really are the bread and butter of our business, which makes sense since we're on the same street as Vera Wang's well-known bridal salon at 73 Newbury Street. We've developed a strong partnership with her salon over the years and now refer brides to each other more often than not. And I've worked quite a few of those weddings.

I always adore working on weddings. The love and the joy is simply contagious. And everything is always just so pretty, no matter where the wedding is held. Heck, I've seen weddings and receptions in backyards that outshine the ones at ritzy country clubs. Of course, anyone who hires us has money to spend and the dollars to turn their backyard into the reception from "Father of the Bride".

Oh, that movie -- the Steve Martin one, not the one with Elizabeth Taylor, even though that one was also beautiful. I still laugh at the wedding planner, Franck, in that movie, and the swans, and still bawl my eyes out at the end (years old spoiler alert!) when she calls from the airport just to say goodbye, since she'd missed being able to say "thanks" to her dad before heading off from the reception due to a series of mishaps. What can I say? I'm a sap. It's not too surprising I wound up working for an event planner.

And speaking of my job — It's not like I don't know what I'm doing. I do. Over my years at Ellerbee Events, I have produced countless weddings; Bar and Bat Mitzvahs; Sweet 16 parties and more with Ashley's guidance. Plus, I'm now a certified Event Planner. Certified. Not certifiable, although there is that, too. But this... This is the first event that I'll be managing without Ashley there. Eek. Deep breaths.

If only I had known that the process of producing the event would be the least of my worries...

CHAPTER 2

Thankfully, I will have help, as we always do for all of our events. Ryan will be there along with Travis Landry and my dear Kitty, the other Event Planners.

First, there's Kitty, who is one of my best friends. She started a year after I did at Ellerbee Events, so we feel like we've been through the event planning trenches together. We are so Mutt and Jeff that of course we had to become best buds, which proves that old adage right that opposites attract.

With a height of 5'10" and an average (aka a few pounds more than I'd like) figure, I consider myself like an Amazon. However, my hair is just below shoulder-length and light brown instead of the long flowing almost black locks of most Amazons on TV. I also steer clear of oh, leather bodysuits or bodices, and instead always dress pretty conservatively in various tones of black and grey, with nothing too tight or revealing. Anything that doesn't draw attention to me at all, helps me to blend into the background, and hides my curves at the same time is fine by me.

On the other hand, Kitty is this cute, petite woman who defines herself as a "lipstick lesbian" and sports very light blonde hair that she always wears in pin curls. She mainly wears bright vintage clothing in Rockabilly and 50s styles when she's not working; corsets, hot pants, long black or white gloves, and garter belts with thigh highs when she's up on stage performing; and pencil skirts and vibrant-colored sweaters when she's at work.

While I try to fade into the woodwork more often than not due to social anxiety that kicks in at the most inopportune times, Kitty always finds herself (or more aptly -- "puts" herself) front and center in a crowd. She loves the spotlight and she can have it, which is fitting since she moonlights in a Burlesque troupe as a singer/dancer. I've been to a few of her shows for support and she absolutely rocks it. Kitty is a person who was meant to be up on the stage. She's so self-confident and it overflows when she's performing. Me? I'll happily sit in the crowd far away from the spotlight and cheer her on.

Kitty has been such a great friend. Before I met her, I was a shy little mouse who wouldn't speak up in work meetings at all even if I had thoughts to share on new things to try at events — which I did — thanks to thinking no one would want to hear them. With Kitty's guidance, help, and the confidence her friendship gave me, I started speaking my thoughts and ideas and, to my delight as well as utter shock, I found that Ashley actually liked and even relished them.

There's nothing I enjoy more than getting together with Kitty for a night of gab sessions at my house or her apartment with wine, chocolate, or pizza (or all of the above) to discuss our romantic travails and life in general. Those nights usually wind up with us dancing like complete goofs to "Walk Like an Egyptian" by the Bangles or "And We Danced" by The Hooters, which we think of as "our song" as we first bonded over how silly we were dancing and twirling away to it one night that we were hanging out. We always have so many laughs when we're together, but we also know we can turn to each other when things aren't so funny, too, which of course happens in life. It's just nice to know I can count on her and she on me during both the funny times and the sad ones.

Heck, Kitty even got me to do karaoke once -- albeit at her apartment instead of up on stage in front of strangers. But I must admit that I did have fun caterwauling my heart out to Carly Simon's "You're So Vain". My love of that song doesn't take too much figuring out, considering the on-again off-again relationship I'm in with a guy, Spencer, who is, when I think about it, really, really vain.

Kitty keeps threatening to take me to a karaoke bar to sing in front of a crowd as the next step in my road to confidence-building. I jokingly told

8

her I'd be okay with it as long as Carly Simon's songs are available, but she wants me to branch out further and start out with a duet with her of "Lady Marmalade", the Spice Girls' "Wannabe", or something like that. It's funny because I'm actually not all that opposed to the idea now. Even just a few years ago, that thought would have horrified me.

Okay, maybe starting with another song would be better, however, because singing about asking someone to spend the night with me, even in French, or about them becoming my lover, might be a bit more than I can handle my first time singing in public. Thankfully, Kitty understands that and has deigned to consider "Mamma Mia".

As L.M. Montgomery coined in a book I loved when I was growing up, "Anne of Green Gables" (but where is my real life Gilbert Blythe?), Kitty is truly a "bosom friend" of mine and she has brought out the best in me. I'm certain that if I hadn't met her, I still would be a meek little lamb who never spoke up and had no self-confidence at all. Knowing her has changed me for life, and I'm so glad we found each other as she's basically the sister I never had.

As for Travis… Well, where do I begin? He started at Ellerbee Events a little over a year ago and caught my eye immediately with his windswept wavy reddish hair with a long curly section that swoops down over his right eye; hazel eyes; his striking good looks; mischievous grin; his penchant for wearing three-piece suits, complete with a buttoned vest (I adore that look) for work meetings, and his height of 6'5".

Okay, I hate to admit it, but I'm kind of a heightist. I've only ever mainly been attracted to guys that are taller than me, for no good reason at all except for wanting to be with a guy who makes me feel little since I feel too tall and big for the world most of the time. This also explains my guilty pleasure crush on Dog the Bounty Hunter, since I'd look petite next to him. It's not like I've turned down guys who were my height or shorter, but my eye has always been drawn to guys who were taller.

I do sometimes wonder if Mr. Right is out there but I've passed him by because he was my height or shorter. Heck, I've certainly met enough of the Not-Even-Remotely-Mr. Right guys, including Mr. Off-Again, On-Again Spencer. That particular Not Mr. Right was someone I knew all too well and that Kitty had heard about all too often, God bless her.

Anyway, back to Travis. I was attracted to him at first sight, but didn't act on it for four reasons.

1. I thought he was gay and I just don't have the right equipment to try and make that work. I mean, come on, it didn't even work when Elaine on "Seinfeld" tried getting that really hot gay guy to switch teams. What chance do I have?
2. Hellooo -- anxiety doesn't exactly lend itself to going up and asking someone out and especially not someone I'll have to see every day at work. I learned that lesson when I did somehow summon up some crazy amount of courage I didn't know I possessed in high school to ask out a hot coworker at the local department store to the prom of all things as a teenager and learned he had a live-in girlfriend and baby. Awkward! Back into my shell I went after that embarrassment!
3. I was seeing someone (the previously mentioned Not Mr. Right) off and on.
4. I made a rule for myself to never date coworkers -- except in my dreams, apparently, where all bets are off, as are all clothes. Damn those dreams.

Well, turns out my gaydar absolutely sucks since Travis asked me out over instant message a few weeks after he started working at Ellerbee Events when we were joking around about something. Whoops. Didn't see that coming. Thankfully, since it was over instant message, he didn't see me blushing like a fool and I was able to just go with my rule about not dating coworkers. He did take that explanation really well and we've become friends since then. Heck, he's even gone out with me, Kitty (and Ryan, when he joins) on our coworker outings, and has been to my house and Kitty's apartment for group movie night.

During those nights out when it's just me, Kitty, and Travis, I've found out that, despite my lack of self-confidence, I'm one hell of a wing woman when it comes to hooking them up with people. Who knew?

I really love when either of them meets/ends up going home with someone while we're out that I somehow make happen by chatting the person or one of their friends up. Yes, you read that right. I actually go up to people for my friends and start up conversations, because I know I'm potentially helping them find someone they could hook up with/date.

Heck, that right there shows me that I'm fine with being just friends with Travis and don't secretly want anything else. If I was interested in him as anything other than a friend, it would kill me to see him leave with someone or even hear him talk about someone, and I sure as hell wouldn't be going up to women to try to set them up with him. There would be an instantaneous flash of jealousy and hurt, and I've never felt that with anyone Travis hooked up with or dated.

I definitely can recognize jealousy when I feel it because I used to tell Spencer that *of course* I wanted to hear all about his dates and the girls he was pursuing when we first started out as friends back at college. Mainly because it meant he was talking to me. However, honestly, it tore me up to hear about them at all because I wanted him to be interested in me, and I spent many a night crying myself to sleep after he told me about the latest girl. Masochist, party of one right here. With Travis, however, I'm genuinely happy for him and want to hear all about any dates.

"Yoo hoo! Earth to Maura. Come iiiiiiin, Maura", said Kitty, interrupting my reverie.

"Crap," I thought, flushing. "How long have I been not listening and did I say anyone's name out loud?"

CHAPTER 3

"Maura, where the heck were you just now? I've been saying your name for a few minutes to get your ideas on the Winter Dance" teased Kitty. "You seemed a million miles away. Looked like it was somewhere fun, though, considering that faraway smile you had plus that blush."

Dammit. I could feel myself reddening even more as she said that. "Oh, you know me -- always off in la la land imagining the way conversations should have gone long after the fact," I laughed, quickly covering.

"Well, that la la land looked like an ooh la la land" chuckled Kitty. "I hope you weren't daydreaming about that asshole Spencer, though, and if you were, do NOT tell me, since I don't want to know. Well, okay, I'm lying. I totally do want to know and I'll just give you an ass-kicking in my head. But not right now. You can tell me all about it over wine this weekend."

I grimaced, knowing all too well that she wouldn't let this one go and would want all the lascivious details later. I could easily spill about the daydream of a hot day and sweat dripping down abs, but just replace Ryan with my on-again, off-again, whatever the hell he was buddy Spencer. That would be a lot easier to explain and wouldn't be all that much of a lie since lord knows Spencer has played the starring role in many of my daydreams.

"Okay, okay," sighed Kitty. "I know that look. No fun story time for Kitty right now. Harrumph. Fine. You'll tell me later and now it's back to reality. So, any ideas for a different name for this thing than 'The Winter Dance'? It sounds like a high school dance. Blech."

"You're right," I replied. "And as much as I think the donors would love to relive their youth -- and probably pay good money to do so -- it's really more of a winter fundraiser with dancing and a silent auction rather than just a dance since the point is to raise money for the historical society. But maaaan, that sounds like a stodgy snooze."

This year's winter dance/fundraiser/whatever the hell we wind up calling it is for the top donors (aka those with the deepest pockets) of the Massachusetts Historical Society and is being held at the old Adamson Manor in Concord, which is the sole building in Massachusetts that closely resembles the Newport Mansions in both size and grandeur.

Despite not being used for formal events for decades, the mansion was in great shape, having been kept up by the proprietor, Wilford Huntley. He opens up parts of the mansion during certain months for tours that are always well-received -- especially the "Haunted Happenings" ones thanks to ghostly legends that surround the mansion.

"Hmm, can we hype up that whole ghost thing?," asked Kitty. "Maybe call it the Dance of the Dead or Some Horrific Evening? Okay, I'm kidding. Well, kind of. Okay, not really kidding at all because I'd go to that second one in a hot minute and now I want to go find one or create one!"

"Oh, crap! Please don't call it either of those anywhere, even jokingly," I pleaded. "The last thing I need is to remind anyone that people were killed at the last event that was held in the mansion's ballroom in case they somehow haven't already heard about that. Oh, maaaan. Remind me again why I wanted to have it there. What was I thinking? This is going to be a freaking disaster!"

"You wanted to have it there because you fell in love with the place on first sight, you silly goose," Kitty reminded me.

She's right. I certainly had. Located far back in the woods off of Route 2A, the Adamson Manor is at the end of a road that winds through the woods leading to a circular driveway with a large fountain set in front of the grand double doors. Large windows set on each side above the door make it seems like eyes are watching you approach, but it's far less creepy than it sounds, or at least it is for me. It's almost soothing and comforting seeing those windows there waiting for you as if they want to make sure you arrived safely. The stunning roofline features turrets with one on each side, giving it the appearance of an old English castle. How could I not swoon at the sight?

When I first saw the mansion and the grounds for the first time in person, including a garden featuring stone statues -- but thankfully no angel statues (Thank you, "Doctor Who" for introducing me to the Weeping Angels, which cause me to now look askance at any stone angel statues) -- when I was on a tour, I got goosebumps and had the strangest feeling that I'd been there before and even had a flash of being at a party that was held on the lawn and then dressed up in finery and dancing across the floor of the ballroom during a grand ball at the mansion.

I shivered, but brushed off the sensation, presuming that I'd been there on a class trip as a child or something and didn't remember. Hell, it wouldn't be the first time that had happened. This feeling had come to me previously when I went to Castle Hill in Ipswich for a company retreat. Standing in the Rose Garden and looking up at that exquisite mansion seemed so familiar to me that I seriously thought I'd been there before as part of a past life. I could see myself taking a casual stroll along the grounds dressed in clothes from the Roaring 20s, having a kiss stolen in that very garden, and then attending a lavish party inside. Hell, it was so vivid that I even began to read up on past lives to see if I could learn more about it or figure out a way to see if it was true that a past version of me had lived there at Castle Hill.

However, those fantasies of discovering information about a previously unknown past life were later dashed when I was flipping through the TV channels one night and caught "The Witches of Eastwick" (the Jack Nicholson movie, not the TV series, which was nothing like the movie) again and realized that it was filmed there at Castle Hill. Light bulb moment occurred. That is why I recognized it. Aha. Well, that explained that... No past life as a debutante at Castle Hill for me. Sure was a nice fantasy, though. So, the same must be true for the Adamson Manor, even though a quick online search hadn't turned up any TV shows or movies filmed there.

We'd actually originally planned for this fundraising event to be held at Castle Hill, but they were booked for the night that the Massachusetts

Historical Society wanted and refused to budge on. Fortuitously enough, I received an email flyer about the tours at the Adamson the same day we were trying to figure out a new site. Strange, because I'd never heard of the mansion before that day (which was surprising since you'd think a mansion of that size would have come to my attention in my research) and didn't recall signing up for their mailing list.

This is a usual occurrence, though, since my email address often winds up receiving email promotions that I'd forgotten I'd signed up for at tradeshows or on websites. That's the joy of working in event planning. I'm constantly attending shows and researching online to sign up for any and all information I can get my hands on regarding locations or companies that might be beneficial to us down the road. So, I get to learn about all sorts of unique properties. Since I look at so many possibilities online each day, I'm sure I signed up for this without even remembering it and it just happened that the flyer went out the day I needed it. That's probably what happened here, even though the name wasn't ringing a bell. And, hey, the timing sure worked for me.

After lunch that day, I went on the tour and fell head over heels for the mansion. It was just stunning -- from the magnificent grand staircase featuring a rich red carpet (imagine the dramatic event photo opportunities for the guests! They'd really feel like they were making a grand entrance on that red carpet) with ivory and gold balustrades nestled between floor to ceiling ivory and gold pillars in the open two-story foyer to the rich Oriental and Persian rugs throughout and the hearth-warming fireplaces in the sitting rooms both upstairs and downstairs and all of the bedrooms. Not to mention the formal dining room and the breakfast room.

I felt immediately at home walking around and taking everything in and even stole away back into the foyer during the library part of the tour (the room I wanted to see the most, so you know I must have been overly excited by how perfect the mansion was to miss it!) to call Ashley and tell her all about the location. I knew that the library would be there waiting for me to enjoy all by myself when we went back for our prepping day before the event, as long as Ashley was fine with using the site, which I was sure she would be, so I didn't feel too bad about missing out on the library during the tour.

Of course, the main attraction for the Winter Dance guests would be the ballroom. It filled the majority of the back of the first floor of the mansion and featured a sparkling chandelier, a wall of floor-to-ceiling windows that looked out over the back lawn, and a large dance floor. Well, at least that's what I'd been told by Wilford.

I hadn't seen even a glimpse of the ballroom yet for myself, because that room was the only one that was closed off on tours. But I was dying to see it when we opened up the room to prepare for the Winter Dance. Even without seeing it, I could picture it in my head quite easily just from descriptions and from the little reverie I'd had about dancing in it -- which I was sure wouldn't quite match up when I finally saw the ballroom. How could it? I just hoped I wasn't in for a bad surprise when I finally saw the room in person. Ashley would kill me if it was a mess.

The elderly tour guide, Wilford, was also the mansion's proprietor and caretaker, so I spoke with him after the tour and my call with Ashley to book the mansion for my event. When Wilford, who had a full head of bright white hair and a sharp, pointed nose on a kind face, and I were talking in the downstairs sitting room with a portrait of the Adamson family hanging on the wall, I asked him why the mansion wasn't being used for events all the time when it was so gorgeous and just the perfect setting for a wedding, party, or any other event. That's when I found out about the mansion's ghastly past.

"Oh, people are just too superstitious," shared Wilford. "The last event that was held here was a wedding reception back in the 1940s. The Adamson family was rich and very well-known, so they were able to get the Ink Spots to perform live, which was quite a coup back in the day. The Ink Spots performed 'I Don't Want to Set the World on Fire' as the song for the couple's first dance -- but during that dance, the main chandelier in the ballroom came crashing down, killing the newly joined husband and wife instantly. Since then, everyone talks about how they think a ghost caused the accident and the room is haunted."

"How horrible!," I blurted out. "That poor couple -- all ready to start their life together and then to have it tragically end like that? But surely people don't think a ghost really caused that? Come on. Be straight with me. There was a loose wire or screw in the ceiling, right? And you're just saying it was a ghost to drum up publicity for tours of the mansion -- which hey, is fine by me."

"That's the funny part," said Wilford. "The investigators examined every inch of that chandelier line and didn't find anything that could have possibly caused it to fall. So, the crystals and lights were replaced and the chandelier was hung back up. But reports from the reception guests all say they swore that no one was near it and some of them claimed to have heard a haunting yell right after the chandelier fell.

"Since then," continued Wilford, "folks have shied away from having any events in the ballroom here because people think they hear yelling and laughter, so we keep it closed off to the public to be on the safe side. But it's been long past time for some light and non-ghostly laughter to return to that room, so we'll happily open it up for your event. If we're lucky, your event will be the one that brings everyone back and ends superstition about the Adamson Ghost once and for all."

"Eep," I thought. "Well, I hope this doesn't put a damper on the RSVPs and that Ashley's okay with it."

Thankfully, Ashley was thrilled when I showed her the pictures of the mansion and the website the next day at the office and dubbed it perfect. When I told her about the chandelier falling during the wedding reception, she was horrified for a moment, but quickly laughed off the notion of a haunting at all and said it would be fine.

"We all know people are morbid as hell," Ashley declared. "They'll come out in droves to see if by any chance they encounter or hear a ghost and then they can sell their exclusive story along with videos/photos to the tabloids."

She was right, as usual, and the RSVPs came pouring in. I wondered if people were more curious than anything else to fully see the ballroom in all its glory (I know I was!) but whatever got them there was fine by me as long as nothing happened while we were there. We currently had 150 people registered for the fundraiser and even had to start a waiting list in case there were any last-minute cancellations.

Plus, it's been close to 70 years since the last incident. If there was a ghost, wouldn't something else have happened in that time frame besides random tour-takers just thinking they heard a laugh? Surely any ghost would have gotten bored and moved on by now. Or whatever kept that ghost there would have been destroyed given all the time that has passed. Right?

There I go again trying to convince myself everything will be okay. I really should have been spending the time convincing myself to find another location.

CHAPTER 4

Right before Ashley left for her flight to Europe to manage that Kardashian wedding, I grabbed some time with her in her office to go over my ideas for the Winter Dance. The majority of our office was sleek with a modern, techy look in tones of gray, black and white, which makes me blend in quite a bit -- just the way I like it -- since I dress in the same colors. Ashley's office, however, was more in tune with all things to do with romance than high-tech. It was decorated in lavish shades of pink and ivory, which was also her personal style. I don't think I've ever seen her wear any other shade, now that I think about it. Even today she was wearing a pink pantsuit with a ruffled ivory blouse.

That romantic theme resonated throughout her office with plush furniture, throw pillows and even pink and ivory furniture. Ashley's desk itself was ivory with pink knobs on the drawers. I settled down in the plush pink loveseat, moving some ivory fur pillows around so I could sit comfortably, put my legs up on the pink ottoman, and started telling Ashley all about the event.

"Okay, so the theme you decided on is 'Some Enchanted Evening'," mused Ashley as she checked in for her flight on her iPhone. "Please tell me that you're going the classy, elegant Cary Grant movie-like route and not like we've taken a time machine back to a 50s' sock hop with pink and black polka dots on the walls and tables and the catering staff dressed up like wannabe greasers for the men and poodle skirts and scarves for the women. Talk about an overused theme! I just had flashbacks to my high school

19

prom themes." Ashley stopped and shuddered, her light blonde hair swinging off and on her shoulders as she moved. "Oof. Bad memories. I mean, my dates were always hot, c'mon, but that is such a ridiculous and overdone theme."

"Oh, Ashley, you know me better than that," I said, knowing she was joking. "Don't worry. It's the first one. Pure, classic elegance. I'm actually envisioning twinkling lights everywhere. I want the guests to feel like they've entered into a world that's ablaze with light -- as if they're on the walkway of the Concourse in Washington, DC connecting the East Wing of the National Gallery of Art to the West Wing. When someone is on that walkway, it is the most beautiful scene because they are just surrounded by lights everywhere. Lights are above them, below them and all around them as they walk through the Concourse. This will be the same. There will be lights around the double doors at the entrance, along the banisters of the staircase, and throughout the ballroom, with luminaries set along the floor to lead them from the lobby back to the entrance of the ballroom. Rope lights will even guide the guests as they drive up the winding road through the woods from 2A to get to the valet parking at the circular driveway at the mansion. The lights will be sporadically placed at first, but then will be continuous starting halfway up the drive, so they'll get that feeling of emerging into the light right from the start."

Ashley glanced up from typing away on her classic BlackBerry phone, envisioning the light-strewn mansion and driveway in her head. She couldn't live without both her iPhone and BlackBerry and said that composing emails was just easier on her BlackBerry but she also needed the functionality and camera of her iPhone. She sure was hitting the keys quickly for whatever email she was writing now, but she was smiling, so it must have been a good email. It was most likely an email or text to Ryan, I guessed. Hell, I know I'd be smiling if I was messaging him.

"That really sounds lovely and especially perfect for this time of year," said Ashley. "I'm sorry I'm going to miss it. So, tell me more. How will the tables look and the rest of the décor?"

"The walls in the ballroom are a very pale yellow from what Wilford told me. They're almost gold in color in the sunlight, but the color would pretty much fade away at night for the dance," I said. "So, Ryan's team is creating billowing white panels that will cover the majority of the walls and then he'll use up lighting throughout the room to bathe those and the other walls in white, silver and a very pale blue throughout the night. Swaths of sheer tulle with white string lights will drape out from the chandelier across the molded ceiling from the painting in the middle for a further starry night effect. We also have gobos of the Massachusetts Historical Society's logo to project onto the dance floor and the walls.

"The tables will be draped in floor-length white linens with a crystal blue overlay, and the chairs will also be covered in white with a pale blue bow around the back of each," I continued. "I want the guests to feel like they've walked into a twinkling winter wonderland, but without having to deal with potentially treacherous driving in snow."

At first, I had also considered having lights surrounding the dance floor for a further luminous effect. It sounded stunning in theory, but then all I could picture was one or more of the guests tripping the light non-fantastic, tumbling down and breaking a hip. Not exactly what I wanted -- nor did our insurance company -- so the gobos, tulle and string lights plus the wireless LED lighting would have to suffice for the dance floor itself and the lights would remain everywhere else. I did look into renting an LED lighting dance floor to put over the ballroom's flooring, but decided that I wanted to preserve the look and feel of the mansion as much as I could. Of course, if I went in and the flooring was crap, then I'd be renting a floor cover on the immediate, but hoped that wouldn't be necessary.

As I told Ashley about the details, I could see the scene unfold before me. The wait staff would be decked out in classic black and white tuxedo-like attire, presenting the guests with plated hors d'oeuvres, including bruschetta (my personal favorite); mini Beef Wellingtons with Béarnaise sauce; asparagus tips wrapped with Prosciutto; bacon-wrapped scallops; and mini pizzas. A table would be on prominent display in the middle of the foyer for the cocktail hour, featuring an ice sculpture boat overflowing with shrimp, along with fresh vegetables, cheese, and crackers on the side.

Dinner would be food stations, starting off with a salad station; followed by a carving station of prime rib and turkey with vegetables; a fajita station; a pasta station (have to have a non-meat option) with cheese tortellini and penne; and a mashed potato bar, which was becoming increasingly popular at events. For dessert, guests could indulge in dipping strawberries, pieces of pound cake, or sliced bananas into a chocolate fountain; a sundae bar; and a candy bar -- a table covered with glass containers filled with different candy, along with little boxes to hold their favorite treats to enjoy later.

My mouth was salivating at the thought of all of that delicious food. As my mind was pondering that chocolate fountain, I guiltily thought of Ryan's muscles and how they'd look with chocolate dripped on them to be licked off inch by inch by delectable inch.

I brought my mind back quickly back from that train of thought and realized there was something I needed to ask Ashley and hoped I could do so without seeming too nosey. "By the way, why isn't Ryan heading with you to Europe? It would be a great getaway for you guys. Plus, you could get married or even just elope over there. I'm sure you could find such a picturesque location for your wedding."

Ashley looked visibly startled for a second, but thankfully not upset. She then said "Oh, honey, you need Ryan here to help with all the construction details and production work for this event. We want it to go off without a hitch! Plus, it just simply makes more sense for him to stay in the States. He'd be bored off his ass in Europe because I'd be so busy with the Kardashians and they already have a full construction crew there, anyway. And, speaking of that, I have a plane to catch to meet up with the crew to get going. Hope the Winter event goes great. I want all the details emailed to me along with pictures galore of how it all looks, my dear! And if you encounter a ghost, get that shit on film so we can be the ones to sell the coverage! Tootles!"

With that, Ashley winked, blew me a kiss, and swirled out of her office to jump into the waiting limo to take her to the airport. She looked like she had something more on her mind that she wanted to talk about before she left, but I presumed it was just the details of the celebrity wedding taking up space in her brain and that she'd sort it out on the long flight across the Atlantic and send me many emails about it. Part of me selfishly hoped that her flight wouldn't have in-flight Wi-Fi available, so I could relax and not feel pressured to answer a flurry of emails tonight.

When I was done with everything I needed to do at the office, I jumped on the Green Line of the T at Copley and rode the subway to Park Street, switching over to the Red Line there for the rest of the journey to my usual stop at North Quincy Station. Per usual, my car was nearly the last one in the parking lot thanks to my long hours. I happily sighed as I sat down in my car, turned on the heat (heated car seats were the best purchase I ever made!) and blasted my 90s mix CD. I couldn't wait to head home to my cozy cottage, eager to get some rest and relaxation before the very busy prepping session of the next day.

CHAPTER 5

My home was my personal oasis away from the craziness of work and life in general. It was a homey two-bedroom cottage right across from the scenic Wollaston Beach in Quincy. Whenever I entered my house, a calm feeling washed over me as the light blue walls, sheer white curtains, and my seafoam green coach came into view. Plus, I had my mom's now vintage Lane hope chest as my coffee table.

My parents had gifted the hope chest to me when I graduated from high school. I treasured it as it had first been my mother's. She received it when she graduated from school and had used it to store blankets, baby clothes, and precious belongings before passing it along to me. Now, I loved seeing it in my living room daily and it gave me a sense of peace just seeing it there.

Okay, so having the water right across the way sure didn't hurt in always making me feel better as well. I had purposely decorated everything to mimic the look of being on Cape Cod, where I had spent many fun, relaxing summers with my parents growing up.

As much as I wanted to head straight to the computer and check email to see if Ashley actually had sent anything from the plane (I'd already responded to her limo emails from the office before leaving), a relaxing bubble bath was calling my name first. I quickly shed my clothes, tossed them into the awaiting white wicker hamper, and headed off to bask in warm water and bubbles in my clawfoot tub in the bathroom.

That tub was one of the main reasons I bought my house as I'd previously had just a walk-in shower at my apartment and longed for a tub. The bathroom with its pale gray walls and dark gray tile floor did also contain a glass-doored shower stall with a white tile surround. Having both a tub and a shower in the bathroom of a house this size was indeed a rarity, as there typically wouldn't be room for a tub as well. However, the previous owners had done some renovations to the house when they lived there, tearing down the third bedroom to widen the bathroom and install the tub. I absolutely loved the sheer decadence and relaxation of having the tub, although I took a shower most mornings just for the sake of time.

And yes, Amazons can indeed take bubble baths. I can't submerge my whole body under the water, though, so either my knees or upper torso wind up out of the water feeling cold whenever I try to take a standard bath without bubbles. This is why I'm a big fan of bubble baths. If I get the bubbles high enough, they can often even cover my knees, which makes me feel tiny -- not at all my normal feeling.

I poured some unscented Epsom salts into the tub along with a capful of Mr. Bubble extra gentle bubble bath. The bath salts do wonders for easing away stress and any aches from sitting at my desk all day, but they don't create the necessary bubbles, which is why I add in the bubble bath. When the tub was finally ready, I sunk down into the almost too hot water, sighed and laid my head back against the carefully placed and secured tub pillow. I had thought about bringing a book into the tub with me, but didn't want to risk dropping it into the water and decided resting my eyes and fully relaxing was the better choice by far.

I closed my eyes and enjoyed the tranquility along with the water and bubbles combining to lap against my skin making me feel like I was floating on waves in a pool or inside a float tank, minus the extreme claustrophobia that experience would cause me. For a while, I did indeed forgot for a few moments about the stress of the fundraiser and everything I had to get done the next day at the Adamson Manor.

Since I'm human, quite a few daydreams also flitted through my brain about Ryan, Spencer, and hot actors while I was relaxing in the tub, but I was so zonked from the planning that I shooed them away so I could simply enjoy getting some rest. The bath was so relaxing, in fact, that I almost dozed off.

Just as I thought I was about to fall asleep, I used my toes to turn the lever and open the drain to awaken me. Trust me, one is far less likely to fall asleep in the tub with the water rushing away from you down the drain, since it causes one heck of a chill.

After I had moved over to the shower to wash off any remnants of the bubbles and bath salts, I put on my fluffy leopard-print robe (the one item in the house that doesn't quite match the seaside feel, but I love the robe too much to care) and grabbed my iPad to sit on my bed and have some mindless fun playing Candy Crush after checking my work email.

My bedroom also evokes the Cape for me with walls painted in Sherwin-Williams Sea Salt (a very pale blue), sand-colored throw rugs covering the hardwood floor, and white blinds covered by light gray linen/cotton Pottery Barn curtains that came with blackout liners. Perfect to block out the sun when I wanted to sleep in.

Ashley hadn't sent any messages alerting me to an issue in planning or anything else, so that was a relief. I clicked over to my Gmail to take a look at the latest promotional emails there in case I felt like some online shopping therapy. Nothing caught my eye this go round -- for which my bank account would be very happy -- so I went to close the window. Just as I was about to hit the x to close the screen and move to matching up those damnably addictive candy pieces (I was up to level 981 -- which shows just how little of a hot social life I have), a message popped up in Chat.

When I saw who it was from, I wished I had closed down Gmail just a second sooner, so I would have missed the message until tomorrow.

CHAPTER 6

It was from Spencer Jacoby -- that guy I had dated/was seeing off and on and just couldn't quit thinking about. Normally, it would have been great to hear from him, except that I was realizing more and more that he didn't seem to care a whit about me unless he wanted something or was lonely or both.

Spencer and I had gone to college together. He was (and still is — that bastard) quite hot, but in a bookish, college English professor kind of way with blonde hair that's swept back from his forehead; a cocky smile; steel grey eyes, and a perpetual hint of a mustache and beard that just looks like he decided not to shave, but instead is a look he works to achieve daily. He also sports hot glasses that he actually doesn't need, but he thinks they make him look smarter. It's all about appearances for him, and I had sure fallen for that look by hook, line, and sinker.

By luck of the draw, we were placed in the same dorm Freshman year and had a number of the same classes together, so we would always wind up walking back and forth from the dorm (which was a trek from campus — great on gorgeous spring and fall days, and not so great on rainy or snowy days) at the same time and started talking on those walks. We became friends with a bit of flirting here and there along with an occasional night out at the movies, but nothing ever came from it besides friendship and me getting to hear all about the women he'd date. Oh, so fun. Plus, I was an overly self-conscious timid little mouse back in college -- even more so than now, as unlikely as that might seem -- so that didn't help. After college, we went our separate ways, but then we reconnected at our 5-year reunion.

The minute he saw me at reunion, he came right up to talk to me with a big smile on his face like he'd been waiting all night for me to arrive. That made my night as Spencer had a way of making me feel like I was the only person in the world any time he was talking to me. When his eyes met mine, it was like there was no one else in the world he'd rather be talking to or spending time with, as he's so laser-focused on just me when we're together. That feeling is certainly good for the ego.

Of course, I didn't realize at the time that that's how he is with every single person he's around and wasn't just a special way he acted only when he was around me. That undivided attention goes to whoever is there — it's just his usual state of being. This is probably why he's so successful in his software sales career because he makes the potential customer feel like any offer is one he created especially for them.

That night we re-met, however, that attention was such a turn on and made me feel unique and wanted, which was a true rarity for me.

You know how models always claim to have gone through an awkward stage growing up and then they blossomed into the swans they are now? Well, I'm not calling myself a model, nor even a swan at all, but that awkward stage growing up? Oh, yes, I had that in spades. However, I still feel like I'm in that stage and I never grew out of it.

Despite being long, long rid of the Coke bottle lens glasses, braces, and overall gawkiness that I was teased about quite a bit as a kid (or which probably developed because of that teasing. Never sure which was the chicken or the egg in that scenario…), I still see myself as someone who isn't beautiful nor even pretty and certainly not someone guys would be interested in. I'm not the kind of woman that guys would turn their head to get another look at on the street nor come up to speak to at the bar or at a party and I've always accepted that.

Heck, I refer to myself as an Amazon in a completely self-deprecating manner. I know that a tall not even remotely size 2 woman isn't for everyone. That's not exactly something that is often seen as a desired trait in

a love interest according to the guys I knew, nor in TV or the movies --
Xena and Wonder Woman and their hot outfits notwithstanding as true
Amazons.

And, yes, I know some people can get past childhood insecurities with ease,
but I'm not one of them. I wouldn't go so far as to say I'm ugly, although
there have been moments where I really have had moments of thinking
that, despite my best girlfriends telling me over the years I'm absolutely
pretty. Blame a guy who I overheard say "woof" when he was talking about
me on the phone to a friend, while I was knowingly in hearing distance.
Yeah, ouch. And also, who does that? The guy was totally an asshole
looking back, but it still stung. Even without that comment, I just don't see
myself as all that attractive.

And honestly, why would any guy be interested if that's how I feel about
myself? The saying goes that you get what you send out, right? So, my
feelings about myself are probably sending a big ol' "Go away" sign to any
true potential love interest around me at all times or a big blue light special
to any creeps out there looking for women with low to no self-confidence.

Seriously, it's like creeps have special vision goggles that show them the
women that don't feel good about themselves and make those guys present
themselves as the "knight in shining armor" that the woman needs. But the
real truth is that, as the saying goes, that knight in shining armor is just a
douchebag in tin foil. Shiny, yes, but the guys try to either make the women
into who they want them to be or just mistreat them horribly. At times, I
wonder if there really are any good guys out there thanks to my years of
getting hit on by the absolute jerks.

I heard from so many brides-to-be that came into our offices to plan their
weddings that they met their fiancé online, so of course, yes, I gave online
dating a shot and signed up for Tinder, Match, and Bumble. I did get a
response, but it all seemed to be so meaningless. I had coffee with a couple
of guys I met online over the years and always had such high hopes after
great messages/texts with them all. However, each time in person, it was
always just so different and the chemistry was never there and conversation
didn't flow like it did online. Even when I thought it did, they clearly didn't
as I'd get the "I'll text you soon to make plans" never to hear from them
again. Just didn't seem worth it for someone who deals with insecurity and

rejection issues. Not to mention the quite unwanted dick pics that would sometimes even show up as the first message. Pass!

Due to all of that hefty baggage, having Spencer's rapt attention was a heady feeling for me. I invited him back to my hotel room that night after the reunion for drinks, which isn't my usual style at all. I think it's easy to tell that I have no moves, but inviting him over felt right because it was Spencer and we'd known each other since college. Also, unlike my usual, we wound up sleeping together that night.

No, he wasn't the first guy I'd ever slept with -- a friend from high school was my first a few years after college. However, that experience was just "okay". Let's just say fireworks didn't go off at all and I certainly wasn't hot and bothered by it. Hell, it felt like I was kissing a relative and being around him just never did anything for me. Yuck. Not attractive at all, I know. So I didn't feel a need to repeat that again with anyone else as I didn't see the appeal in sex from the experience.

With Spencer, however, I got it. I understood why people liked sex so much because damn, it was hot and made me want more and more and more. Even thinking about that night -- and every time with Spencer thereafter -- makes me hope he'll be back again soon. We spent the next day together (most of it in bed with one very fun romp in the shower) and went out for dinner that night and then wound up in bed again after back at my place.

I was still naive enough at the time to think that, of course, we would start dating after a night, day, and night like that, but that wasn't the case. Spencer said he'd had a great time and wanted to see me again, but then he dropped off the face of the planet. A few months later, out of the blue, he texted me "hey" one night and we got to talking and he came over so he could vent about his day and we wound up sleeping together again. And then he went into ghost mode again.

I know. I know. I really should have stopped talking to him right then and there because, c'mon, ghost mode is a big no. Hell, anytime someone ghosts Kitty -- which isn't often, but it does happen -- I'm the first to tell her to ignore the guy if he ever comes crawling back. I just can't take my own advice when it comes to Spencer, though.

So, it became a thing. Whenever Spencer was feeling lonely or bored, he'd send me a text or message to say "hey", that he missed talking to me, and wanted to see if he could come over and talk/vent about his day. Then, we'd wind up sleeping together again and then he'd disappear again for a few weeks or months. This pattern repeated itself each and every single time over the past five years and I just let it keep happening. Who has a big L on her forehead for letting this demeaning pattern continue? Yes, this girl.

I did have Spencer come up as a potential match on Tinder once and swiped right on him, thinking he would do so as well when I showed up on his possible matches and we'd have a good chuckle about it. Nope. Never got the "match" notification about him, which was disheartening. I don't know if I ever actually did show up as an option for him, but I'm assuming I must have, especially since I'd swiped right on him, so I'd show up sooner in his feed, and he just swiped left. Lovely.

Yet, I always held out hope that one day Spencer would suddenly wake up and realize that I was the one for him and he didn't need anyone else and he'd show up at my door as a big romantic gesture with chocolate or some tulips. Why not roses? Well, I'm weird in that I don't really like guys showing up with roses. In fact, I kind of hate it. That always screams "trying too hard" to me or as an apology for something they did. Plus, c'mon, "The Bachelor" and the whole "Will you accept this rose?" thing really killed them for me as a flower.

To no one's surprise, though, that's not reality and Spencer has never once shown up at my door with flowers or chocolates anyway. Yup, I'm a naive little twit. That is never going to happen. Over the years, I have tried to cut things off for good a few times, but I keep getting lured back in thinking this time that he's changed.

When I saw that Spencer had dashed me a message saying "Hey", my hopes ran high yet again that this would be the time that was different, and I wrote back instantly with "Hey there". I let my emotions get the best of me and was so excited to tell him about the big event I was planning on my own as we hadn't talked in a while. In my heart of hearts, I thought that maybe my planning this event all on my own would be what finally prompted him to see me differently -- as someone who was a leader and self-confident and worthy of him. Worthy of him? Seriously? I'm such an ass. Where is my self-confidence?

As I started typing about the event, I saw that he had already written back to vent about how tough his day was and how things weren't going right at work, which was a pretty usual occurrence for Spencer. Despite his success as a salesperson and his outgoing personality, he always thought that people at work had it in for him and wanted him to fail, which I never understood. I guess I am lucky that I enjoy my coworkers and know we all have each other's backs, so I really don't get thinking that people actually want something bad to happen to you or thinking negatively all the time.

I did feel sympathy for him, because that's no way to live, but also had more than a twinge of sadness and even anger (it was about time!) from not being able to share my happy news in place of having the conversation be all about him and me needing to be there for him again. So, I sucked it up and swallowed my excitement, offering sympathy and letting Spencer know I was here if he needed to talk or wanted to come over to vent. He vented for a while without really replying to anything I was saying -- he might as well have just been typing to a wall or copying and pasting something he'd written verbatim to someone else -- and then he typed "BRB".

Now, to most people, that acronym truly means "Be right back" and the person does come right back to type again/continue the conversation after stepping away for a moment to answer the phone, or let the dog in, or use the bathroom. To Spencer, however, I sometimes think "BRB" must really mean "Be real, babe" or something akin to that kind of brush-off message, as he then proceeds to not come right back and instead drops off messenger for a day or two without any explanation or care.

Knowing this (I guess I have learned at least something over the years), I waited online for just three minutes to see if he came back, but then logged off. No need to look even more desperate than I probably already do by sending him a bunch of messages to find when he next logs onto Gmail. Ugh. Why do I keep doing this to myself and let him get to me/use me like that?

When will I finally meet someone who will pay attention to me and actually be interested in what I have to say and how I'm feeling/how my day was and want to talk to me instead of at me? Or, actually, when will I be able to honestly say "goodbye" and mean it to someone who doesn't care a thing for me except as some plaything that's always there patiently waiting for him to pop up and give him the attention he craves? It's way past time.

With Spencer, it's always about him and what's going on with him. Thinking about it, he's never once asked me how I'm doing, except if he's hoping to hear some interesting story about a client or wants me to tell him I'm thinking about him all the time. Hell, he's probably off right now listening to some other woman that he is interested in, making her feel like she's the center of the universe now and paying attention to her because he got the attention he wanted from me, which is all he ever wants. I really need to find some strength and move on.

Heck, this is probably why I've been having the daydreams about Ryan -- because he IS committed to someone already, so I know that he actually does have that ability to do so and stay monogamous. I'm assuming that last bit, of course, but I think I can safely say Ashley would have dumped him in a hot minute if he wasn't faithful. Hopefully he's just been winding up in my fantasies because he's the representation of what I want and seems to be one of the true good guys out there. Maybe it's not really him that I lust after, but the idea of him... Yeah, I have a bridge to sell myself...

Oy. It's well past time for me to move on from Spencer. I mean when I think about it, it's been five years of this. That's horrifying when I tally up all the time I've basically wasted on him. Not to mention the money I've spent on sexy lingerie for those rare nights with him and food to cook to try to show him what a great girlfriend I'd be if he'd just let me. Suddenly, I felt very embarrassed and sad for myself over the whole situation and started crying.

Needing to do something to get over feeling that way, I logged back on to Gmail. I found that Spencer was still listed as being offline despite saying he'd BRB (again, no surprise there), so I steeled myself, took a deep breath, and sent him an email saying what was in my heart and what needed to finally be said:

"Spencer~ I'm really sorry you had such a rough day, but I can't stick around as your backup plan/shoulder to cry on anymore. I had a really great day and wanted to tell you all about it because I'm so proud of myself and what I've been accomplishing at work. But I felt like I couldn't tell you because your day was the only thing that mattered to you. You didn't ask how my day was at all, but then again, you never do. All you wanted to do was talk at me about your day. I need someone who wants to know about MY day as well as talk about their day.

"I don't want someone who just wants to listen to me blather, but I don't want someone who's going to just talk at me like I'm a wall. I hope you know that I really have loved our time together. You are absolutely amazing. And I do care about you, but this can't continue because I need more.

"Hell, I deserve more. I need space and time away from you to focus on me. Please don't call me or contact me. I do wish you happiness, but I also wish that for myself and I can't find that happiness if I'm still in touch with you because I'm honestly too addicted to talking to you. But I've finally realized that you can't give me the true relationship that I want, so I need to find it elsewhere."

With my heart racing, but feeling a profound sense of peace for finally getting that out there and being very straightforward about the whole thing, I hit "send". Yes, I could have called him to tell him that or told him face to face, but I always find I communicate better in writing, and honestly, I chickened out, knowing that hearing his voice would have swayed me into not saying what I wanted to.

Plus, Spencer has a great voice. It definitely works for him when he makes sales calls. So masculine and just compelling. He's sure compelled me -- without meaning to -- to keep staying addicted to him instead of leaving him behind over the years , not that I didn't enjoy every moment...

Okay, stop it. No more thinking about Spencer. I hit send on the email. It's out there, so it's done and for real this time. Glancing at the Chat, I saw that Spencer was still offline. Dammit. I was hoping that he'd be "green" (online) so I'd know that he would be seeing my email sooner rather than later. Oh, well. Nothing I could do about it now.

Thankfully, I had some ZzzQuil in the house for those nights when I knew that my mind would be wandering or I made the mistake of having caffeine after 2 p.m. (never a good idea that), causing a sleepless night. I took a dose of it and crawled into bed, letting my head be caressed by my double pillows (one firm, one soft, which combines to just right for me) and pulled the insanely comfy duvet cover over my head, closing my eyes to get some sleep. I did fall asleep easily, but a blissful night's sleep was not in the cards.

CHAPTER 7

"MOM! DAD! Noooooooooo!!" I jolted awake, gasping for breath with tears running down my cheeks and images of a burning car seared in my head.

Those nightmares had haunted me ever since the night of my Boston College graduation, when my parents, Mark and Sarah, were killed in a car crash. They were on their way from their hotel in Newton to pick me up at my apartment in Brookline (I lived off campus senior year) for a celebratory post-graduation dinner when a drunk truck driver ignored a stop light as he was coming onto Route 9 and drove straight into my parents' car, causing their car to burst into flames.

When the buzzer sounded at my apartment that night, I merrily flew down the stairs without bothering to call down and check who it was first, since I was expecting to see my parents' beaming faces behind the glass door. Instead, I was stopped dead in my tracks when I saw the police officer who was standing there to deliver the brutal news.

I was told that my parents had died instantly, but in my recurring nightmares they were still alive for a few minutes after the crash, screaming from the torture of the flames hitting their skin, coughing from the fumes and smoke billowing inside the car, and desperately trying to get out of that burning car. In my dreams, I'm always stuck helpless outside of the car yelling and frantically trying to get to them by breaking the window or pulling open the car door to no avail. Why wouldn't that nightmare go away? When would it end?

Damn that survivor guilt. I still feel like if I had been with them, they wouldn't have been killed because they would never have been on the road at that moment. I know. I know. I'd seen a number of therapists since then and each one told me that it wasn't my fault. Some even added that if I had gone with them directly to the restaurant after the ceremony, we could have been coming back from dinner and wound up in that same moment at the same time with the drunk driver. And in that case, I'd most likely also be dead now.

But it's tough to not think about the "What ifs?". What if they'd taken just a few minutes longer getting ready? What if they had left just a few minutes earlier? What if I hadn't gone to grab drinks with friends? What if that driver hadn't been drinking, someone had taken his keys, or he had hit a pole before arriving where my parents were driving? What if I'd taken a taxi cab to the restaurant to meet them instead of having them drive to get me? The guilt just wouldn't go away.

There were plenty of moments in the days and weeks following their deaths that I wished I actually had died, as I loved my parents so much and the thought of living without them and not being able to talk to them ever again wrecked me.

On that night of my graduation ceremony, I had made last-minute plans right after the proceedings to get together for drinks with my girlfriends while Mom and Dad went to their hotel to grab a nap and change into more comfortable clothes before coming to pick me up back at my apartment for dinner. To this day, I kick myself for not inviting my parents along for drinks. If I had, they wouldn't have been on that road at that moment in time and would most likely still be here. Yet another "What if?".

In our last conversation after the ceremony, Mom had given me a huge hug, told me how proud she was of me, how much she and my dad loved me, and mentioned that they had some news they wanted to share with me at dinner. I wish she had told me right then and there what it was as I still wonder what that news could possibly have been.

I think I can safely say they weren't going to announce that Mom was pregnant since that would have been a bit out of the blue at her age, although not entirely impossible. Mom had always said that they thought of having a second child, but it just never happened, so they stopped trying (not that I want to think of that -- everyone thinks their parents are asexual, right?). And they always seemed perfectly fine with just having one child, especially at the holidays, when they'd wonder how parents who had multiple children paid for gifts.

Wouldn't that have been a shock, though, if Mom was pregnant and I was going to have a younger sibling? Aww, I would have been a great older sister, I think, and would have been able to help my younger sibling to learn from the many errors of my ways and to not do what I did dating-wise. Plus, if it was a girl, I could have bought all the cute little girl clothes for her and helped her with makeup, or really she probably could have helped me with makeup and fashion instead.

Okay, dumbass. Stop it. If that was the news or not, you'll never know and you're not going to suddenly have siblings now. Keep that line of thinking for buying cute little clothes for if and when you have a child down the road.

Plus, I would think Mom and Dad would have mentioned a pregnancy to me privately instead of telling me at dinner while we were in a crowded restaurant. Maybe they were planning to stop off at their hotel room to tell me the news before dinner.

However, it was far more likely that they were going to take that cruise they had always dreamed of now that I had finished college and they had banked time off at their jobs (Mom was a librarian and Dad was a book editor -- they always loved discussing their jobs. Mom got an inside look into what books were coming down the pipeline and Dad loved hearing what types of books library patrons were requesting and borrowing) and saved up money over the years. The thought that they never got to go on that cruise they'd talked about all their lives still slays me. Such unfinished lives.

On the good side, my parents did have a long time together anyway, since they were high school sweethearts. Scratch that. That's when they had officially started dating, but they'd really known each other since kindergarten and were each other's first kiss back then when they were playing "Sleeping Beauty" with Mom as Sleeping Beauty and Dad as her Prince Phillip. Their first kiss location wasn't a glass coffin in a thorn-covered castle but was instead at the top of a slide, which was serving as the glass coffin. Mom loves telling the story of how Dad kissed her and she was so startled that she couldn't keep her balance and slid down the slide. How adorable, innocent, and sweet is that?

Yes, they had dated other people in middle school and early high school, but after they officially started dating, there was no one else but the other for them. They truly only had eyes for each other. Heck, their song was "I Only Have Eyes for You" by the Flamingos.

They were my role models for what I wanted in a relationship -- Mom and Dad always looked at and spoke to each other with love and tenderness. Even when they were having minor disagreements, it was still clear that they loved each other and were just squabbling instead of being disappointed in or truly angry at the other. I knew without question that despite how long they had been together as a couple, there had never been anyone who caused one of them to look the other way. It would have shocked me to my core if that was the case. They certainly enjoyed spending time out with friends and socializing both individually and together, but they were also quite happy just having a simple night at home with each other and me.

It sounds old-fashioned, but I loved that my parents truly did love each other and actually relished hearing how the other's day had gone over dinner. They seemed to just love hearing the other talk and wanted to know every detail of every story they told. And they shared that love and interest with me. My lack of self-confidence is all internal and had nothing to do with how I grew up -- I knew that I could do no wrong in their eyes and that I was loved by them no matter what.

In these days of casual hookups, one-night stands, and cheating galore, a relationship like that of my parents sadly seems to be a thing of the past. However, I still hold out hope that I'll find a love like that. Or that time travel will be invented so I can go back in time to a decade when those relationships were far more common and I can meet the man of my dreams at a country club dance while dancing the night away to jazz tunes or at a sock hop. First, I probably needed to finally get away from Spencer, as he was not going to be that person to me. After that email I sent tonight, I hoped we really were done and I wouldn't relapse, so I could find a love like my parents had.

After the tragic deaths of my parents, I took a year to cocoon and grieve the loss of my only family. I know I was lucky that, thanks to a quite unexpected inheritance from my parents (which I hoped wasn't the cruise money they'd been saving up for years), I didn't have to work for that year and could instead take the time I so desperately needed to myself. I was able to look for, find and purchase my now home for solace, be alone, cry, rant and rave, and over time, learn how to live life without having them around to turn to whenever I wanted. To this day, I still go to pick up the phone and start dialing my parents' number to talk to them. It's agony each time to realize halfway through hitting the numbers that they're not there. I'm not sure that reflex and the pain that comes with it will ever go away.

Around a year after their passing, I started looking for a job that would help me take my mind at least somewhat off of my loss. Plus, I needed money to live, of course, and knew I'd be happiest getting back to work. I needed a position I could throw myself into -- one that would be time-consuming and require dealing with a lot of minute details, so I would have something to focus on. Getting the job at Ellerbee Events gave me exactly that. And boy, did I ever find what I was looking for -- and also found some horror I didn't see coming.

CHAPTER 8

After that night of not-so-great sleep, I got up and threw on my trusty Old Navy Rockstar skinny jeans. Thankfully, pre-event prep days didn't require my usual simple but classy work attire of a gray or black sheath dress (I love not having to coordinate a top and pants or blouse and skirt) with a blazer or cardigan on top, depending on weather. So, jeans it was along with a deep red tank top under a matching cardigan finished off with a pair of cognac-colored knee-high riding boots.

I left my hair down for once and blew it dry instead of having to deal with a million pins to wrangle it up like a herd of cats into my usual sleek chignon or ponytail. All that was left was to put on some BB cream (I could kiss those inventors for making getting ready so easy and for the ability to hide the circles under my eyes after that not-so-great night of sleep), blush, eyeliner, and lipstick and I was ready to hit the road, carrying a travel mug of coffee straight from the Keurig with creamer -- the perfect start to what was sure to be a busy planning day.

I was the first to arrive at the Adamson Manor and as I pulled into the driveway, my phone chimed alerting me to a message. I grabbed the phone to see if anyone from the team was running late and groaned when I instead found a text from Spencer that simply said "Hey".

"UGH!," I muttered to myself. "Seriously?! Are you kidding me right now with this shit? I am so not replying. Come on, dude. Leave me alone. Did you not read my email last night? I know I didn't send it to the wrong person, since I double- and triple-checked the 'to' line before sending. Okay, so Spencer, tell me... are you trying to see if you can make me forget I sent that email so you'll still have me to run to whenever you need attention? If not, what the eff is this? Baaah! This is my day to shine and plan this awesome event -- not to have to deal with more of your freaking mind games."

Feeling fed up, I tossed my phone into the backseat to get it as far away from me as possible so I wouldn't be tempted to reply. Irony reared its head as Olivia Newton John's song, "Hopelessly Devoted to You", came onto the radio as I threw my phone. "Ah, you're so very funny, fate!", I chuckled. "Wrong, though. No longer hopelessly devoted to that unworthy schmuck."

Okay, so I did feel like I was being a bit overly bitchy and letting Spencer dangle wondering why the heck I wasn't jumping like Pavlov's dog to respond at the chime of a message from him, which I usually did, despite my email to him last night. Hell, one time I was charging my phone and didn't notice he'd sent a text until 20 minutes later. He actually sent a follow up text asking me if I was okay because I didn't reply right away as he was used to that. Aaargh.

Okay, breathe. This is a good thing. Let him mull on my not replying for a few hours. He might actually realize I mean business with what I said in my email. I decided to leave my phone in the backseat and not bring it in the house with me. That way, I wouldn't be swayed to text him back at all in a weak moment. Plus, it would probably be good for him to be knocked down a peg.

And yes, I realize this is all bravado and absolutely wishful thinking. Spencer probably wouldn't even notice I hadn't replied yet and is probably ignoring what I said in my email, knowing that he's gotten me in the past to come back by giving me attention/focusing on me for just a day and then reverting back to his old ways. I can't let that happen this time. I won't.

Plus, if I did apologetically reply later with "So sorry I missed your text, yadda yadda yadda", he'd just write back that it was no big because he'd forgotten that he even texted me. Yup, could already see how that would go, and then I'd feel even worse because I'd been brushed aside yet again. Not happening. I've been down that path too many times.

So, that phone was staying in my car. No need for any more texts from him (including, heaven forbid, any texts where he would proclaim his love, because I think I've finally realized that isn't going to happen, although I wouldn't put it past him to try so as a last-ditch effort to keep me wound around his little finger) to throw me off base on this insanely important day where all my focus was needed on the planning.

I turned off the car and stepped out feeling strong, confident, and ready to take on the day (all rare feelings for me), only to swiftly felt a chill straight down to my bones. I've always heard that means someone is talking about you, which okay, would be valid since any of my colleagues could have mentioned me in telling someone their plans for the day. But then the thought of the rumored ghost danced through my head.

"Stop it!," I scolded myself. "It is the beginning of December after all, so cold weather isn't exactly surprising." Still, that unexpected chill left me feeling a bit disconcerted because it looked bright and sunny out, with just a few Bob Ross-like puffy clouds hanging in the air. I shook my head to brush the uneasy feeling aside and reached in my pocket for the key Wilford had given me to unlock the double doors. Once I had entered the foyer, I found that the heat was certainly working inside, so that helped to further dispel that cold chill I'd felt on arrival.

Looking around at the magnificence of the foyer from the sparkling marble flooring to the rich, vibrant paintings on the walls, I couldn't believe my luck that this gorgeous grand mansion would be the site of my first ever solo planned event at Ellerbee Events. I was so happy at my good fortune that I let out a squeal and did a dance of joy complete with a "Yes" chant just like the WWE wrestler Daniel Bryan. Yes, I do watch wrestling on the rare occasion. There are a lot of tall, hot wrestlers, including Kevin "Diesel" Nash, who first caught my attention with his height of over 7 feet tall and those muscles, so I watch. I was so giddy that I spun around and around with glee with my arms out in the air -- somehow without feeling dizzy, thankfully. I continued spinning until I heard a deep chuckle from behind me.

CHAPTER 9

I spun around towards the door to find Ryan leaning up against the open doorway watching me with a shit-eating grin on his face and a steaming cup of Dunkin Donuts' coffee in his hand. He was wearing an unbuttoned denim blue button-down shirt over a white undershirt with a small tuft of chest hair peeking out, and black cargo pants. How did he make such a casual outfit look so damn appealing?

"Dammit! I didn't hear your car drive up. How did I not hear that? Do you have a special silent car or something? Did you sprint silently down the driveway? How long have you been standing there?," I stammered, turning bright red from embarrassment. Of all the people who could have caught me being such a freaking goof, it had to be Ryan? Why couldn't it have been Kitty at the door? She would have also laughed, but with me instead of at me as I feared Ryan had -- and Kitty would have happily bounced on over and danced and twirled right along with me without question instead of standing there. Ugh. How embarrassing!

"Long enough," chuckled Ryan. "I don't think I've ever seen you let loose and enjoy yourself like that before. I've seen glimpses of it here and there, but I'm surprised this isn't how you are when we're all out. Wow. That was entertaining and surprising as hell. You should have fun like that more often. It sure suits you, as does the color of that top, which is currently matching those very attractively blushing cheeks."

Flushing even further, I cursed myself for not being very witty with a comeback. I'm sure I'll come up with a great one at 3 a.m. tomorrow morning. It will be ever so helpful then… I had no idea at all how to respond nor where to even start with that. It sure sounded like he was flirting with me, but there's no way that could be the case since he's engaged to my boss and it also just didn't seem like something he'd do.

Sure, Ryan had always been pleasant when we were working together or hanging out, but I'd never detected even a hint of flirtation before today. Hell, maybe this was just the way he was, though, and I'd never picked up on it, although I like to think even I would have noticed that.

Or, maybe he was secretly really like Spencer and was just lonely and bored as Ashley was out of town, so he decided to flirt with me since I happened to be standing right there in his line of sight. Great. That's just what I needed. Yet another Spencer in my life now that I'd finally decided to be rid of him. Fabulous. I really didn't want to think Ryan was anything like that, but was beginning to realize I might not know even one little thing about how men think and act.

I didn't have to ponder those thoughts too long as Kitty and Travis came bursting through the doorway into the foyer, cracking each other up with tales of their separate adventures the night before out on the town with their dates. They screeched to a halt in silence when they saw Ryan and me standing there.

"Umm, hmmm… Hi there, you two. Did we interrupt something here?," Kitty quickly asked, noticing the mortified look and blush on my face along with the still-present smirk Ryan was sporting.

"No. Certainly not. Nothing at all," I stammered, putting back on my professional mask of authority and picking up the papers I'd set aside on the staircase to pass out to the team. "Since we're all here now, let's go ahead and get started. I have a checklist for each of you of the timeline leading up to the event. We can head into the women's formal sitting room to sit down and go through it to make sure nothing's missed."

Kitty, Travis and Ryan followed me silently into the room, which was located to the left as one entered the foyer. This was the formal sitting

45

room for the women of the house and their female visitors. The formal sitting room for gentleman was positioned directly above on the next floor, which was standard practice for the time in which the manor was built and decorated. Heaven forbid men and women socialized with each other in the same room back then. That would have been scandalous!

The showcase of this sitting room was a polished mahogany baby grand piano with a pair of plush soft pink loveseats (Ashley would have loved them for her office!) in front of it on each side. A large fireplace also served as a focal point with an almost life-sized portrait of the original Adamson family set above the fireplace against the floral wallpaper.

The portrait depicted the family in a common pose for sittings back in the early 1920s. Wilford had mentioned the names of the family during the tour and, quite surprisingly, they'd stuck firmly in my memory. The parents, Edward and Emma Adamson, were seated in two chairs with their children standing between them. Edward wore a formal dark suit befitting the occasion of the portrait and Emma had chosen a complementary high-necked dark dress. In contrast, the children all wore white or ivory (it was tough to tell the actual color from the sepia-toned portrait) with dresses with dark bows for the girls and short pant suits for the boys with dark vests.

The eldest daughter, who looked to be in her mid-teens and was standing next to her mother, was named Elizabeth. A bow set in her hair appeared to be trying but failing to keep her flowing ringlets from becoming unruly. Their eldest son was named Henry -- he looked to be about a year younger than Elizabeth. The youngest son, Stephen, who was around 8, stood next to Henry, and the wee toddler, Dorothy, was perched on her father's knee.

In most family portraits from this time, the patriarch of the family gazes forward from the picture without any trace of amusement in his eyes and almost no expression at all, or with a stern one at most. But, Edward did no such thing. In fact, from the portrait, I'm not sure he would have even know how to look stern if he ever wanted to. He had a twinkle in his eye and seemed just so kind and jovial that I could easily see him playing Santa for his children at Christmas and flying them around the air for hours on end as my dad had done when I was a child. Funny how you could get a glimpse of someone's personality just from their eyes even in a portrait.

When I'd first seen the portrait during the tour, his sparkling eyes had caught my attention, so I didn't pay as much attention to the rest of the family. Only now did I notice that Emma was the one with a stern, almost disapproving countenance in the photo. The children, on the other hand, were all perfectly poised with the sweetest smiles, so Emma's angry expression was even more noticeable in comparison to that happiness. How on earth had I missed this during the tour? Now that I thought about it, I could swear that when I first saw the portrait, Emma was smiling sweetly just like everyone else. But that couldn't be the case, could it? Portraits don't change.

"You're losing it," I silently scolded myself. I made a mental note to ask Wilford if he knew anything more about the family history the next time I spoke with him, although I certainly wouldn't ask him if Emma had been smiling in the picture previously. He'd most certainly think I'd gone daft, which I was half-convinced I was. I also hoped that the next time I glanced at the portrait, Emma wouldn't have gone back to smiling, because I'd truly think I was bonkers then.

Since I felt a bit strange with the portrait there, like Emma was scowling down at me, I chose to sit on the couch directly to the left side of the fireplace with my back to the picture so as to not see her in my line of sight. Kitty, in her bright pink sweater and black pencil skirt with matching pink/black stilettos (count on her to dress up even on a casual day and look adorable doing so), curled up on the piano bench since she felt at home there as a performer. Travis chose the other loveseat and sprawled out for comfort, relaxing and putting his feet up on the cushions -- not that his Henley shirt, jeans and Converse sneakers didn't already look quite comfortable. That left Ryan to sit on the remaining loveseat with me. Well, that wasn't awkward at all after the flirtation, ridicule, loneliness or whatever that was out in the foyer. Nope.

Giving my attention firmly back to my checklist, I went down all of the details with the team. Kitty would handle making sure the wait staff knew where to be the day of the event and that all the food and drinks were being taken care of by the catering staff; Ryan and his construction team were going to set up the gobos, wireless LED lighting and up lighting as well as the white draped panels for the ballroom walls inside and the lights to be strewn around the door and the driveway outside; while Travis would help set up the tables and linens with Kitty and me and also serve as point-person with me for any last minute issues that arose from the guests, staff, or otherwise.

"Even though this has all the work of a wedding reception, I'm so glad it isn't one," chimed in Travis, playing absent-mindedly with the skin above his upper lip like he was smoothing a mustache. "They're the worst! You wind up dealing with bridezillas, vendors gone rogue or worse, missing, and crazy themes up the wazoo -- not to mention bitchy bridesmaids who never give me their number."

"That's because they're all giving me their numbers instead," purred Kitty, holding up her phone with glee. "Ooh, there's one of them texting me now. Aww, don't be jealous and pout. You're just not their type, darlin'. I am."

"I knew it!," laughed Travis, playfully wiping his hand across his forehead in relief . "Well, thank you, Kitty Kat. Now my not-so-fragile ego has been appeased. I will rest easy tonight! But still, weddings! Ugh!"

"Oh, don't be so cynical," I replied. "I just love weddings. Come on! How can you not love them? They're so romantic. Can't you just picture the head table draped in linen up in front of those panoramic floor-to-ceiling windows; a band playing swoon-worthy music; the smell of the bouquets, centerpieces and delicious food wafting through the air; and the bride and groom gazing adoringly at only each other during their first dance with love in their eyes…"

"As a large chandelier crashes down killing them both," Ryan sardonically interrupted. "Yeah, that's the stuff of dreams right there."

"Hey! Watch it. Just because you're so soured on love, weddings, marriage and all that," shot back Kitty, "don't take it out on Maura."

She looked like she was going to add something else, but was quieted by Ryan almost growling at her, "Shut up, Kitty. You don't know what you're talking about."

Kitty never backed down from an argument, but by the look on her face, it seemed like she felt almost guilty for saying what she had. That was new!

What the hell was that about? Was something going on with Ryan and Ashley's engagement? Was it over between them and I somehow hadn't heard?

I can't say that my heart didn't do a little tango at the thought of that, giving me hope that maybe Ryan actually had been flirting with me instead of mocking me. Hmmm, I'd have to ask Kitty more about this when I got her alone for a second...

Just then, before anyone could speak further, a loud bang filled the air from the foyer. We all jumped up out of our seats at the unexpected jolt, running out into the hall, looking to see what could have fallen to cause the noise. On our arrival, we saw that nothing was amiss and the double entrance doors were shut, but weren't they already closed when we went into the sitting room? Maybe in the embarrassment of that awkward moment, I hadn't thought to shut them and they'd blown closed in the wind, causing the racket. That would certainly make sense. But if not...

Ryan walked over to the doors to open them and look outside to see if anyone had loudly knocked or something had fallen outside to cause the noise we heard.

"What the hell? These doors won't open," he muttered as he tried to open them again and again to no avail. He then got down on his knees to check out the keyhole, lock placement and the door casings, but nothing looked out of place to him. Feeling the need to help, but not really knowing what we could do, Kitty, Travis and I came over and we each tried to open the doors after Ryan stood up. However, it was an exercise in futility.

"I don't get it," said Ryan. "I've worked with countless doors and locks before over the years, but I've never seen ones like this. It's like these doors turned themselves around after we came inside. The way it looks is that they're locked from the outside with no means to open them from in here, which doesn't make any sense at all. No contractor in his right mind would set up doors like that. How did that happen?"

Just then -- as if in answer -- a haunting laugh floated through the air followed by a crash from the sitting room. Running back to where we'd come from, we all stopped short in shock when we saw that the portrait of the Adamson family was now lying face down on the floor with the frame in pieces shattered around it. In the portrait's place on the wall were dripping red words that ominously read "Get out now or you'll die here!"

CHAPTER 10

"Guys, this isn't funny," I shakily said. "If this is part of some kind of sick, twisted joke, please admit it now. Okay, even as I'm saying that, it doesn't make any sense. Besides, how could any of you have done this since we were all out there in the foyer instead of in here. I didn't see any of you dash back in here, so unless one of you has a twin that likes to hide, you couldn't be there and then also be here at the same time when the noise happened. I don't understand it. Okay, and now I'm rambling. I do that when I'm nervous. I know."

I looked at Kitty, Ryan, and Travis and saw nothing but confused looks on their faces. Dammit.

"It doesn't look like it was any of us," declared Ryan, "which means there must be someone else in the house with us who we don't know about."

"Ooh!," chimed in Kitty. "Maybe it's that guy, Wilford, and he'll be wearing a monster mask and when we rip the mask off to reveal it's him, he'll say in a old Western voice that there's gold buried in this here house and he wanted to scare us highfalutin' varmints off to have it all for himself and that he would have gotten away with it, too, if it wasn't for those meddling…"

"Zoinks!," yelled Travis. "As much as I loved the show as a kid -- and I am totally a Fred instead of Shaggy, despite my hair color and what I just said, thank you very much -- you don't really think we're in a Scooby Doo mystery brought to life, do you?"

"God, no," scoffed Kitty. "But wouldn't that be a better alternative than there really being a ghost? Or some freakin' psycho who locked himself up in the house with us for some twisted reason to torture us or lord knows what?"

Couldn't really disagree with that! As we headed from the sitting room back into the foyer, Ryan said, "Let's hope this really is just the work of some random kids messing with us, but first we have to find them."

"Also, we don't really know we're locked in here," I added. "All we know is that the main double doors are stuck, but there are three other exit doors on this floor -- one in the kitchen; another in the back of the ballroom; and then one in the library. And also a bunch of windows that could possibly be opened. Okay, so there was that laugh that can't be explained, and that literal writing on the wall of a warning, but still… Let's check those out and see what's up."

With the ballroom immediately behind us in the back of the foyer, we decided to check that room out first as a group. It seemed silly to split up and go off separately to check the doors in the ballroom, library, and kitchen along with the windows in those rooms, the breakfast room, bathroom, and dining room. Plus, that never works out well in horror movies. We might as well have just ran up the stairs while being chased by the bad guy instead of out the open front door into safety. Oh, wait -- the front door doesn't open anyway… Okay, so we're screwed.

Opening the ballroom door, I jumped, startled by the sound of a high-pitched creaking noise and said, "Ryan, can you put some WD-40 on the hinges of that door before the fundraiser starts?"

The second the words were out of my mouth, I gulped, realizing that there were far more pressing concerns right now than the damn squeaking door -- like getting out of the mansion alive. Ugh! They must all think I'm an idiot, and if Ryan was indeed making fun of me before with that flirting, what fresh hell will this show of ridiculousness bring?

"Sure thing," Ryan said with a quick and surprisingly comforting pat to my shoulder. "You're the boss for this event, so whatever you say goes, okay?"

"Well, if that's the case," I replied, "then I want out of this house! You hear that, house. I want out and Ryan just said what I say goes so LET US OUT NOW!!"

Realizing I was yelling and sounding more than a wee bit panicked, I quickly stopped talking and took a deep breath. Then, I took in my surroundings of the ballroom for the first time and was struck silent by the beauty, as it seemed we all were. From the amazing gilded walls and the gleaming dance floors to the majestic floor-to-ceiling windows looking out onto the sprawling lawn, it was truly stunning. Wilford and his team really had done such a great job of keeping this room up in mint condition over the years. Thank heavens!

It also dawned on me as I looked around that the room DID look quite a bit like the one I had come up with when I imagined myself dancing there back in older days. How bizarre. I know that I hadn't surreptitiously peeked into the windows… mainly because the drapes were drawn tight when I tried to. Hmm, I guess Wilford had done one heck of a job describing the ballroom to me.

"Gosh, look at that parquet dance floor," exclaimed Kitty. "I didn't even know they had parquet back in the 1900s." Kitty knew a lot about dance floors -- both parquet and otherwise -- from all of the ones she had danced on.

"They did," I replied, "but this isn't the original flooring. Wilford told me that the ballroom was first created with marble flooring, but it was tough financially to take care of it over the years. The marble had lost its sheen and had a few too many mars in it from shoes and boots. So, right before that wedding reception back in the 1940s, they tore it up and replaced it with this parquet flooring. That's also when they took apart the wall overlooking the lawn and replaced it with those floor-to-ceiling windows over there to let the natural light shine in for the reception."

When I spoke of the wedding reception, I immediately glanced up at the sparkling chandelier hanging ominously directly above us.

"Hey guys, I found the door," called Travis, who had moved away without notice over to the back right corner of the ballroom. "Remember that whole getting the hell out of here thing?"

We quickly joined Travis over at the double doors next to the stage in the back left corner of the ballroom -- a convenient location to get tables, chairs and band equipment in and out of the ballroom. Oh, freedom and fresh air was so close, I could almost taste it.

Travis grasped the handle on the doors to unlatch and push them open, but the doors stayed shut. I went over and frantically grabbed at the handles, even though that was all for naught since clearly they weren't opening.

I walked over to the floor-to-ceiling windows again, and examined them closely, but didn't see any way to open them, like levers on the sides. It made sense, though, since it's not like they're glass doors instead of windows.

"What I wouldn't give to be out there walking right now," I pondered to myself as I looked sadly out the window. "Even in this cold weather, I would happily take my shoes off to be able to walk through the grass. Hmm, my shoes... Now there's an idea! What if I smashed through the window with my shoe?"

I went to take off my shoe, only to remember I was wearing flat-heeled riding boots that wouldn't do much damage to the windows at all, let alone break through them. "Kitty, can you give me one of your shoes?," I asked. She swiftly removed and handed me one of her 4-inch pink and black heels, seeming to realize my intent.

"Great thinking, Maura," said Kitty. "Maybe we can break one of the windows with my stiletto heel and get out of here." Feeling grateful that Kitty made it a point to always wear heels, I firmly grasped the tip of the shoe and reared my hand back with the heel of the shoe sticking out to hit the glass.

"Whoa, whoa, whoa," said Ryan, grabbing my hand before I could fully swing back, which was good because he was standing so close behind me that I would have hit him in the face. "Before we ring up a large window repair bill or damage Kitty's probably very expensive shoe and then have to replace that, can we try the kitchen and library doors first? Now put the nice shoe down before anyone gets hurt."

Admitting that he had a point, I gave Kitty back her shoe to slip on. Heading out of the ballroom, we went through the foyer past the galley and headed underneath the grand staircase into the other side of the house, which led to the kitchen, breakfast room, dining room, and library.

The cold chill I had earlier felt outside had crept in and filled the air even with the heat on in the mansion, which made us move even faster.

CHAPTER 11

Walking into the kitchen, we hurried over the light gray tiled floor past the black double oven, extra-large steel gray refrigerator, and brand new, gleaming black marble countertops to the door in the back.

"Oh, c'mon, please give us a break and open," I said as I grabbed the doorknob of the bright white door and tried it to no avail. "Dammit!!!"

As I turned away from the door, I felt a bit sick and couldn't believe my eyes. It looked like one of the walls had shifted quite closer to us (and yes, I was having flashbacks to the trash compactor scene in "Star Wars"...) and changed colors in the process from its current cloudy gray hue to an off-white. The light gray tiled floor had also undergone a transformation to a black and white checkerboard patterned floor. What the hell?

I was about to say something to the others to see if they were seeing the same thing, but when I rubbed my eyes, I saw that the wall was back to where it had always been and the floor and walls were the same color as when we first entered the room. Okay, I'm seriously losing my mind. That's just great.

"What the frick is going on in this place!?" yelled Kitty. "Hey house or psycho in this house! Are you bored? You want visitors? Well, there'll be a whole crapload of people here for the fundraiser for you to play with and get your jollies on. But if we can't get out, they can't get in! Now let us out, you twisted asshole!!"

"I'm thinking the point isn't for us to stay here and play or have a party so much as it is to scare us to death or just plain old kill us," said Ryan. "Something or someone in this house hates us, or at least one of us. That can't be good."

"Oh, great," I said. "Now we're each going to be wondering if it's us. That's awesome. Well, for me, the first time I saw this house was when I came here for a tour. Were any of you here before today?"

"No way, no how," declared Kitty. "And once I'm out of here, I'm never stepping foot in here again! You can get someone else to assist at the event, if you even want to have it after today."

"I think I took a tour here on a field trip eons ago as a kid," said Travis. "But that was just a one-time visit and we stuck with the tour guide, so didn't have time to sneak off and conjure up spirits somehow."

"Had never even heard of the place until you booked it," said Ryan.

"Okay, so none of us have some past with the house that we know of," I said. "Clearly, there's something going on, or else this is the work of some total psycho. Not sure I like either of those ideas."

"Umm, guys," squeaked Kitty. "I just saw something go by the window."

"What?!," yelled Travis. We ran over to the window and anxiously peered outside. "Oh, good God, Kitty! That was a freaking leaf. Are you kidding me?"

"Hey, we're all pretty shaken up here, Travis," I said. "Kitty, I would have thought the same thing seeing something outside. Hell, right about now I'm praying that there is someone wandering by outside so they'll be able to open one of the doors for us and let us out of here."

"Okay, let's all try and calm down a little bit," said Ryan. "I know this situation sucks but we will find a way out of here, I'm sure of it. Maura, do you have Wilford's contact info saved on your phone? We can try calling him or even just call 911 to get us out of here if these other doors don't open."

I feigned checking the pockets of my jeans and my purse. "Oh crap, I must have left my phone in the car," I sheepishly admitted. "You guys will have to try 911 instead. Sorry!"

Ryan and Travis pulled out their phones from their pants pockets, while Kitty sidled up to me.

"Wait a minute," whispered Kitty. "You don't have your phone? What's up with that? You always have your phone! You're addicted to that thing and are constantly on it checking it for work emails or to see if there's a text from Spencer the dickhead."

"Ack! Kitty! Don't mention him here," I shushed her as I glanced over at Ryan and Travis, who were thankfully not looking over at us. "Spencer's history, okay? Really. I'm done with him. Done, done, done. I told him last night -- okay, so I chickened out and emailed him last night, but it's basically the same thing -- that I'd had it not being important in his life and that I needed time for me. That's why my phone's in the car. I left it there so that I won't be bothered by him nor tempted to reply to any emails from him if he tries to get me to change my mind. I won't this time. I deserve way better than that shit."

"Oh. My. God. Way to go, sistah! High five!", squealed Kitty quietly, as she put her hand up in the air and then quickly went to run her hand through her hair, realizing Ryan and Travis would certainly ask questions if they saw that and wonder what was going on, as forgetting one's phone isn't typically something to celebrate.

"I am SO freaking proud of you," said Kitty. "That's a big step! I knew that one day you'd be rid of that soul-sucking albatross, and here you are, putting him in your rearview mirror! YAY! You are a rock star! After all these years, you've finally done it. Now don't you dare go back to him. Promise me you won't!"

When I silently nodded, Kitty continued, "Okay, you just absolutely made my day. I've been waiting for you to say that you were done with him for so long! I really want to do a dance of joy, but I won't. However, when we get out of this house, you and I are going out for drinks to celebrate, lady, and to find you a brand new man. Now it's time for ME to be wing woman.

Watch out, boys. Maura is coming to getcha and is on the prowl. Hmm, first, we are getting you some attention-getting clothes. I'm thinking leopard print, and then, meow, here we come!"

"Thanks, Kitty," I said, blushing up a storm. "It really was well past time for me to move on. I mean, hell, it's been five years. Of course, in all honesty, I've been finding myself interested in someone else without meaning to at all. And I need to ask you about…"

"Hey, Kitty!", yelled out Travis over my last two sentences, getting our attention. "Does your phone have a signal? Because neither of our phones do."

"Shit," said Kitty. "I didn't even think to look. Let me check." She grabbed her phone from her purse, and glared at the lack of bars. Walking around the room holding up her phone, she went over to the window. "Not even anything here. What the hell?"

"Okay, so it looks like this is a dead zone," said Ryan, cringing as he'd realized what he just said. "Well, let's go see if we can find another way out or if we can get a signal somewhere else. Maura and Kitty, you two go and try the ballroom doors again. And let's try it without putting Kitty's heel through the ballroom windows or through someone's head, please" with a wink to me. "Travis and I will check the windows in here and in the breakfast and dining rooms, and then we'll look at the library before we all head upstairs if we need to."

"We're on it," I said. "Let's hope one of these options is a way out."

CHAPTER 12

Kitty and I walked out of the kitchen. As we entered the foyer to pass underneath the columns of the grand staircase towards the ballroom, I couldn't resist going to re-check the entrance doors. I ran over to try them again, hoping they'd miraculously open this time. Nope, still stuck shut. Grrr.

"I am soooo taking my heel to that damn window if that ballroom exit door doesn't open," said Kitty as we left the foyer and walked back into the ballroom. "Ryan can go screw if he thinks that…"

She stopped talking as we both stared aghast at the sight before us. The wall that previously featured those exquisite floor-to-ceiling windows was now an exact replica of the other walls in the room, with just gold paneling and not a window to be found.

"Umm, there were windows there before, right?," I asked Kitty. "Please tell me you're seeing this, too. I'm not losing my mind here, am I? Where did they go? What is this house doing to me? I thought in the kitchen that a wall had moved briefly and changed color along with the floor, but this is something entirely different."

"If you're losing your mind," said Kitty, "I am right there with ya sporting a hopefully blinged-out white jacket in the loony bin, sistah. Although minus the kitchen wall thing because I didn't see that. Have no idea what you're talking about there. But this one is right here and I see it in its full freaky ass display of change."

As we continued to look aghast at what used to be windows, I felt slightly nauseated again. "Damn, I think I should have had more than coffee for breakfast," I said to Kitty. "I'm feeling kind of woozy and sick."

"Okay, that's weird," said Kitty. "I am too. Umm, is your vision also feeling a bit off? It looks like everything is moving around me. Did this also used to be a funhouse where the floors moved and Wilford forgot to mention that part?"

I turned my head very, very slowly to try and ward off the nausea, and realized that things actually were changing right around us. The parquet floor had reverted back to its former marble, the tables were all upright and covered in linen and, most notably, there were two women -- an older woman and a woman in her 20s -- now having a tense discussion in the center of the ballroom floor.

"Whoa!," yelped Kitty, walking over to the women. "Where did you two come from? And more importantly, how did you get in here because we need a way out! Hey, pay attention! I'm talking to you!"

Kitty went to grab the arm of the older woman and was startled when her hand went straight through the woman's arm. She then tried with the younger woman and the same thing happened. It was like they were holograms.

"Okay, why can't they hear me and why can't I touch them?," asked Kitty.

"I'm going to go with hoping that this isn't something like that movie 'The Others', which would make us the ghosts here," I said. "Is it possible that they're ghosts? We haven't time-traveled or anything like that, right? Although if we had, we would be able to interact with and touch people, so it can't be that, at least according to 'Bill & Ted's Excellent Adventure' and 'Doctor Who'. What the hell is going on here?"

"Oh, my God," said Kitty. "Wait. I think I know what's happening here. One of my fellow dancers is big-time into ghosts. Seriously. She's created her own Ghostbusters-like team and does haunted house tours. Anyway, she's told me about something called psychic energy. It's when something traumatic occurs at a house. The energy from what happened is captured by the house and is then replayed at any time over and over in a loop. That's got to be what we're seeing. We're viewing some moment from the house's past and it's decided to go full production mode by basically making it look like the house did at the time the event occurred right down to the windows now back to being a wall."

"Aha! That must explain the kitchen wall and floor, because Wilford had told me they renovated that pretty recently with new walls and appliances. Of course I'm not too thrilled with being the quite literally captive audience for this show," I scoffed. "Well, since we're stuck here, let's see what we can learn from listening to these two. Maybe we'll hear something that will help us get the hell out of here!"

We walked closer to the women, who were still speaking tersely to each other. The older woman had a long thin nose, full lips, and dark hair that was fashioned in smooth swept-back rolls along with forward roll bangs -- a style popular in the 1940s -- while the younger woman had long, soft red curls along with stunningly chiseled cheekbones and cupid's bow lips on her beautiful but upset face.

"But Mother, I love him," said the younger woman. "He's all that matters to me and if I can't be with him and have to marry that horrible old man, I don't want to live!"

"Dorothy, you listen to me," said her mother. "Raymond is only 10 years older than you. That age difference isn't that vast. When I married your father, he was 12 years older than me and look at how happy we are."

"Yes, Mother, I know," said Dorothy. "But he's Father and he's so wonderful and kind and happy and always tells us the most wondrous stories. Raymond is just so dull and boring. Plus, my heart belongs to Walter. I know he's not rich like Raymond is and I know what happened. Yes, it hurt me at the time, but now I don't care. I'm sure Walter can explain it all if I am just able to talk to him. He's who will make me happy. And then there's..."

"Hush, now!," said her mother in a lower voice. "Keep your voice down. Don't even speak about that as no one is to know! You will continue not speaking to Walter, put on a smile, marry Raymond, and then he will use his money to help us save our house."

"Oh, you don't care about my happiness at all! All you care about is this house," sobbed Dorothy.

"Well, I guess the show's wrong. Not everyone loves Raymond," laughed Kitty and then quickly stopped. "Sorry. When I'm nervous, I make jokes, and hearing that the guy Dorothy doesn't love is named Raymond brought that straight to mind, so I couldn't resist lightening the mood."

"Thanks for trying to crack me up," I smiled at Kitty. "Hmm, wait a minute. So, her name is Dorothy. She must be the little toddler in the family picture, which means that's Emma, her mother, with her. Holy crap, I wonder if this is why Emma looked so miffed in that portrait."

"Umm, Maura," said Kitty. "What are you talking about? When I saw that picture, everyone looked happy in it. Is this another one of those house is changing things that you saw that I didn't? Although I can't imagine there was another version of the pic hanging up that had the mother looking upset. That would be a weird one to choose to display even for a little while."

"Emma was happy the first time I saw the portrait, too," I said, "but when I saw it today, Emma was almost scowling."

"Okay, that's messed up," frowned Kitty. "It's like this whole house is impacted by whatever happened."

"But this happened so long ago," I said. "None of these people could still be around to write that message that we saw on the wall behind the photo, could they?"

"What I want to know is who she wound up with," said Kitty. "Was it Raymond or Walter or some unknown bachelor number three? Speaking of the Bachelor, please tell me she didn't wind up with someone like Juan Pablo? Ees not okay! But seriously, I can't believe she'd actually want to be with Walter despite my joke about Raymond earlier. If he made her upset, it sounds like there was good reason. Plus, that's such an old man's name."

"It's an old man's name now because it was popular back then," I said, keeping my eyes on Emma and Dorothy, who had stopped sobbing and was now glaring at her mother.

"I did what you told me to do the first time and called off my engagement to Walter after what I saw and now you're going to make me follow your orders again without question," Dorothy said through gritted teeth. "Whatever would Father think?"

"Your father doesn't need to know about any of this," chided Emma. "You know that this is for your father's sake and it needs to happen to save our house since he can't work anymore due to his illness and bills are piling up. He loves this house and it would kill him to lose it. By marrying Raymond, you can do that and make sure that your father is able to die peacefully down the road in the home that he loves. You're our only hope. Elizabeth is married to Thomas, but he can't help since he's a schoolteacher and makes just enough to barely support them. Stephen and Henry could have helped by working, but…" Emma broke off in a sob.

"Oh, Mother," Dorothy exclaimed as she flung her arms around her mother's neck. "I miss them, too. Not a day goes by that I do not wish Henry never joined that bloody war and Stephen never went into the woods on that hunting trip."

"How ghastly," Kitty said. "Their sons must have both been killed. That poor family." She stopped and glanced over quizzically at me. "Maura, are you okay?"

Wiping away tears from my eyes, I said, "Wow. No idea what brought that on. Sure, it's a sad story, but it's not like I knew them."

"Maybe their loss reminded you of your parents' deaths since it's about children no longer being with their parents -- just from a different angle than you experienced," Kitty said softly as she put an arm around my shoulders in a hug. "It's only natural."

"Thanks, Kitty," I said. "That makes sense. I'm sure that's what it was."

We looked back at Emma and Dorothy, who were still hugging and crying. Dorothy stepped back slightly and straightened her shoulders with an air of grim acceptance. "Okay, Mother, I will marry Raymond. We both know I do not love him and never will, but I will try my best to make him happy. And Walter will just have to accept that it is truly over between us. Ohhh, my marrying Raymond is going to break Walter's heart -- and mine -- but I have to do what is best for our family. If only I could tell him about..."

"No, Dorothy!," exclaimed Emma. "That can never be mentioned. Never. No good would come of bringing that up now. It is behind you and you have to move forward. And you do not even have to tell Walter anything at all. Remember, things are over between the two of you. He already knows that, child. In fact, I think he made that perfectly clear. Now, dry your eyes and come with me. We have your wedding plans to finalize." With those words, they went to walk out of the ballroom, but instead seemed to vanish right before our eyes.

At the same time, that nauseated feeling hit me again and the room righted itself into how it appeared when we all first saw it that morning. Kitty and I had to shield our eyes as the sunlight coming in through the reappearing windows seemed so bright after being in the darkened, windowless room.

We tried the door again, but still couldn't get out. Would we ever be able to leave this house?

CHAPTER 13

As we headed over to the library, after checking the bathroom off the library and finding that window sturdily locked, and trying to make sense of the scene we'd just encountered, we bumped into Ryan and Travis in the foyer.

"Well, the windows in the kitchen and two dining rooms were all sealed shut, unfortunately," said Travis.

"Please tell me there isn't a hole made by Kitty's heel in those gorgeous windows," teased Ryan. "It would be the death of me to see those destroyed. We're going to check the library next and then upstairs. Want to come with?"

"My shoes stayed on the whole time, thank you very much," scoffed Kitty. "But, guys, you're never going to believe this!! Those windows were missing when we walked in, the ballroom changed while we were in it, and we saw the mother and one of the daughters from the portrait having a conversation."

Kitty and I filled in Ryan and Travis on the proceedings, and they just stared at us like we'd grown three heads. When we stopped talking and had finished relaying what we'd learned, Travis said, "Attention, looney bin. Special delivery! I have two new patients for you! Seriously, was there some kind of carbon monoxide leak in the ballroom? Because all I can figure is that you guys were hallucinating or else you've been holding out on me and took some acid when you were in the ballroom away from us -- in which case, share with the class and hand it over."

"Seriously, Travis?!," I said. "So, the house is locked for no reason that any of us can see. The windows are also all sealed shut without any explanation. There are threatening words on the wall that seemingly appeared out of NOWHERE, but having psychic energy in the house and us seeing and hearing people who used to live here is where you draw the line in your belief system? Jesus, I'm so glad we never dated and I'm even wondering now why we're even friends! You are being such an ass. Ugh! Unreal."

"Don't talk to me like I'm an idiot, bitch," Travis retorted. "Remember who you're talking to. You and Kitty are the insane ones that claim to have seen the ballroom change in front of your eyes and people show up who died decades ago. Think about it. Who really sounds like the idiot here in this house, huh? It ain't me, sweetheart."

"Hey, hey, hey!" yelled Ryan, stepping between us. "What's gotten into you, Travis? Knock it off, guys. This is no time to be fighting amongst ourselves. We all want the same thing -- to get the hell out of this house. So, let's figure out how to do that. Kitty, how about you and Travis check everything out upstairs, while Maura and I take a look at the library, okay?"

As we went to leave and cool off in our separate corners, I had a sense of foreboding and heard Travis, Ryan and Kitty all groan as nausea hit us. The foyer darkened as the room seemed to spin.

CHAPTER 14

"What the hell?," Ryan said. "I feel like I'm going to puke! Is this what happened to you guys in the ballroom?"

"Okay, okay. Fine. I get it now," groaned Travis. "Really didn't need to have the experience live and in technicolor myself without the joy of drugs. Damn, my head is spinning. I cave. You guys were right. Everything can return to normal now."

As the room righted itself, a large, balding dark-haired man in a long black coat and matching black hat suddenly appeared before our eyes standing in front of the amazingly now open doors.

Before any of us could gather ourselves and try and run out that appealing open door in front of us, we saw Emma come hurrying down the stairs with a bundle wrapped up in muslin in her arms. She went over to the man and gave him the package.

"Thank you for coming on such short notice," Emma said, "but we had to get this out of the house before my husband returns from his doctor's appointment, and before Dorothy awakens from her drug-induced delirium."

"I understand. It's best that neither Mister Adamson nor anyone else know about this," said the man. The bundle made a noise and he moved aside part of the blanket in his arms to reveal a baby's face. "This baby will be well taken care of by its new family."

"Holy shit!," squeaked Kitty. "That's a baby!"

"Thank you, queen of the bleeding freaking obvious," snarked Travis.

"I wonder if Dorothy had a baby with Walter and this is it," I said before Travis could make any further snide retorts. "That would explain the thing she wanted to tell Walter about, but couldn't. But don't you think that she'd put up more of a fight to be with him if she had their child that they could raise together?"

"Thank you, Mr. Wingham, for your help," said Emma. "You will be paid quite handsomely for your silence as no one can ever know that Dorothy was pregnant let alone that she had the baby. Even Dorothy herself can never know that her baby actually lived. She has to believe that it died, which is what I told her before I gave her the Laudanum to make her sleep while I took care of this situation. Thank heavens for my nurse training, so I knew what to do. To be extra clear, no one is to ever know this child lived. Is that understood?"

"Perfectly, madam," said Mr. Wingham as he doffed his hat to her with his free hand and headed out the open door, closing it behind him.

As the door closed, a piercing scream came from upstairs. "MOTHER!!! My baby! My baby is dead!," wailed Dorothy from her room, rousing herself from her delirium.

"Mother's coming. Everything's going to be okay," said Emma, as she scurried up the stairs, and then muttered under her breath, "It will certainly be okay now that the baby is gone, so Dorothy can go on to marry Raymond instead of Walter." The room spun again, bringing everything back to the present day.

I ran over to the door and, of course, it was still shut. I cursed and banged my fists against the door in frustration, but knew that realistically it wasn't going to just have magically unlocked in this timeline.

"We should have run out that door while it was open," said Travis, "and left all of this shit in the past where it belongs."

"We could have," said Ryan, "but who knows where we would have wound up. That door was open back in the time whenever this all happened. When time shifted back, we could have been stuck in the past -- or more likely, just run straight into a closed door that only appeared open to us."

"Ouch, I'm good," said Kitty, rubbing her nose in sympathy at the thought. "I've already had one nose job. No need to have to have another after breaking my poor nose, thanks."

"Okay, guys," Ryan said. "Let's check out the other rooms and find a way out of here. Maura and I will go see if we can open the door in the library. Kitty and Travis, check out upstairs. Maybe there's a balcony with a ladder or staircase out the back that we didn't know about."

"Let's hope so," agreed Kitty as she and Travis headed up the stairs. "I want this place to be something I only see in my rearview mirror as we peel the hell out of here."

CHAPTER 15

Glad to be rid of Travis and his ridicule for a while and away from the disturbing scene in the foyer, but still feeling a bit awkward to be left alone with Ryan, I silently walked off with Ryan down the hall.

"Hey, don't let him get to you too much," said Ryan, sensing my mood and the cause for it, but thankfully not the entire cause. "I know we're all stuck here, but Travis must be taking it worse than the rest of us because he's not usually that flat-out mean. I've never seen him like that before. I get that this situation sucks, but that's no reason for him to take it out on you or any of us, really. We're all feeling a bit on edge here, and don't need his bitching to make things worse."

"It's okay," I said. "Well, fine. Honestly, it's not really okay at all because Travis has never acted like that -- at least never around me before, but I'm going to have to be okay with it and try to keep the peace until we're free and out of here. Things were bound to get tense with us all stuck here right now anyway."

I thought about what had happened in the foyer and felt the need to add, "By the way, thanks for stepping in back there, Ryan. I've never been the violent type at all but I seriously wanted to slap him across the face or punch him -- or both -- for being such a jackass and probably would have if you hadn't stepped between us. That certainly wouldn't have helped matters if I had hit him."

"Well, I'm glad I did," said Ryan. He looked thoughtful for a second and then chuckled, adding "I'm also quite glad that happened there in the lobby and not back in the ballroom when you had Kitty's high heel from hell in your hand."

I found myself laughing at the thought of hitting Travis in the face with a stiletto and the heel sticking out of his forehead. It certainly was an appealing albeit grotesque thought at the moment! Jokingly, I bumped my shoulder into Ryan's, saying "Shut it, you. That stiletto would have made a great weapon if you'd let me use it on him and it sure would have stopped his ranting at least for a few minutes."

It was nice to have things less serious for a moment and I realized that I felt safe and comfortable there with Ryan, despite being locked in the house. Maybe he really wasn't the attention-seeking player like Spencer that I'd made him out to be and he was actually a nice guy. But my intuition wasn't exactly the greatest.

"Oy," I thought to myself. "This is still your boss' fiancé, you nutter. Get a freaking grip. Fine, you can have a crush. Hell, it would be good to get your mind off of Spencer and, admit it, you already have a crush on Ryan anyway -- but don't fall into daydreams of walking off into the sunset with him and having a happily-ever-after together. For Pete's sake, he's marrying someone else, and it's your boss at that, you idiot, and, not to mention, she's a hottie. You're not. He's not going to give you a second thought, let alone a first."

"You okay, Maura?," Ryan said looking over at me curiously. "You seemed like you were lost in your own little world there." He chuckled and continued, "I hope you're not silently plotting to steal Kitty's shoe and stab Travis because orange is really not the new black."

Blushing at being caught in my reverie yet again, I turned my face away to hide my reddened cheeks and changed the topic from what had been going through my head.

"Oh, yes, all's fine," I said. "Sorry about that. I was just somewhere else thinking about Dorothy and Emma's conversation and how Emma had taken away Dorothy's child. It's just awful that Dorothy was being forced to marry someone she didn't love and was also being kept in the dark that the baby she had with the man that she did love, despite some sort of issues with that relationship, was actually alive and well. She and Walter could have had their own happy ending, but that possibility was taken out of their hands."

As he opened the door to the library, Ryan looked thoughtful and said, "I agree with you. That's a truly terrible thought. Being stuck marrying someone you don't love is like winding up with a life sentence in prison with no chance of parole. No one should have to do that. Hell, it's no way to live. I believe everyone should marry someone they truly enjoy spending every hour with 24 hours a day. Now, they don't need all the same shared interests, mind you, because no one should marry a clone, but there needs to be enough there that you don't wind up wishing you were anywhere else or with anyone else all the time."

I pondered his interesting words as we entered the room and wondered if he was speaking from the voice of experience. Could he actually not love Ashley and not want to marry her? I thought they were the ultimate couple, but I also know you never really know what someone else's relationship is really like behind closed doors. Hmm....

Or was I really just reading into those sentences he said and hearing what I wanted to because I so desperately wanted him for myself? Sadly, that was probably more likely, and really, even if something had gone wrong with Ryan and Ashley's relationship, it wasn't like he'd ever be interested in me.

Shaking my head to clear my thoughts and stop focusing on Ryan, I turned to take my first look around the library. I'd missed this part of the tour as I was calling Ashley then to discuss renting the mansion for our event and had been dying to see what it looked like ever since.

It was even better than I'd imagined. If a person had to live forever in just one room, I would choose this one. It was the most exquisite library I'd ever had the pleasure to be in and the English major part of me almost cooed at my dream library being a reality right in front of me. I was surrounded by all of these beautiful old books (the smell of them was heavenly), which lined the shelves from floor to ceiling on every wall.

The only two walls that weren't laden with books were the ones looking out onto the yard through the side panels on the door and the one with the gray marble fireplace. Both of these walls featured rich red mahogany paneling. There was a wheeled ladder up against one of the book-strewn walls -- all the better to reach those books on the highest shelves. I seriously felt like I'd stepped into the library in "Beauty and the Beast" and wanted to start singing.

"Oh my word. I'm fairly certain I've died because this must be what Heaven looks like," I sighed.

"It is quite a striking room," agreed Ryan. "Just look at the workmanship of the shelves, the craftsmanship of that Federal-style door, and heck, even the detailing on that ladder over there. You can tell a lot of heart went into all of the pieces here."

"What first caught your eye seems about right considering what you do for a living," I chuckled. "We're in the most beautiful room I've ever seen, and here I am drooling over all of these amazing books wanting to smell and read each and every one, while you're taking in the woodwork and details."

"You're right," said Ryan. "That is pretty funny. Now, don't get me wrong. I do enjoy reading, but I'm more of a reading on my Kindle kind of guy rather than actual paper books, so the books here on the shelves don't do anything for me. All of these old books actually make me worried about bugs like silverfish that could be hiding in them to somehow eat away at those stunning shelves. In this room, what first draws my eye is the carpentry... and that door over there, of course. Let's go check it out and hope that baby opens."

I reached the door first and turned the handle, which refused to move. "Oh, bloody hell!," I groaned. "Won't one of these doors decide it wants to open? I'm about to say you should hoist me up that fireplace so I could pull a reverse Santa, but I fear we'd find that permanently blocked at the top as well with an unbreakable chimney cap."

"Let me try the door," said Ryan, coming up next to me. "I know. I know. I'm sure it won't suddenly open when I try, but I really want to give it a try anyway and hope it suddenly gives in and opens up to show off that I'm a big, strong, manly man. Okay, I'm kidding. Kind of." He grinned and winked at me, grabbed the handle, and tried to turn it a few times, but unfortunately to no avail.

Frustrated, but not too surprised after our luck in all the other rooms, I walked over to the desk, which was situated in the middle of the library. "This must have been Edward's study at home," I said, picking up an old fountain pen.

As I held the pen, I felt that now far too familiar feeling of being nauseated and heard Ryan mutter "Oh, come on. Now what are we going to see?" as the room begin to spin yet again.

CHAPTER 16

This time, the surroundings of the room stayed the same from what I could tell, but we saw two people coming in through the doorway. I recognized Dorothy from her appearance in the ballroom earlier. This time, however, she looked much happier and a bit younger than when I'd seen her. She was carrying a fresh bouquet of gorgeous red tulips wrapped in a white ribbon and was wearing a slightly below knee-length summery white dress covered with light purple and cranberry flowers, which featured puffed short sleeves and a bias cut, along with cranberry colored t-strap heels. The man she was with wore a white safari-like shirt with tan high-waisted pants. He was tall and built with blonde hair that was slicked back on the sides but curly and unruly at the top of his head.

"Walter! Shhhh. Hush now," giggled Dorothy. "I don't want to alert anyone that we left the lawn party to spend some time together. It's bad enough that you plucked these tulips from Mother's garden and took the ribbon from my hair to wrap them."

"Walter!", I thought. So this was the man that Dorothy loved so much and was the father of her child. Well, no wonder she loved him. He's pretty damn cute and he sure seemed to make her happy from this brief glimpse!

"Oh, my dear Dorothy," said Walter. "You know that you're always safe with me no matter where we are. Although as lovely as you look in that dress, I don't honestly trust myself to be alone with you in this room for all that long..."

"You stop now," laughed Dorothy. "We won't be in here for a long time at all. All I want is one single little dance with the man I love. Is that so wrong?"

Dorothy took Walter's hand and led him over to the Victrola in the corner, which I hadn't previously noticed. I briefly wondered if it would actually still be there when the room restored itself to current day.

She lingered at the Victrola for a moment to gently set down the tulips beside it on the table and put on a record. Then, Dorothy turned to Walter, looking up at him from beneath her long lashes, held out her hand, and sweetly asked, "May I have this dance, dear sir?"

"Well, madam," said Walter, taking Dorothy happily into his arms. "I thought you'd never ask. It would be my true pleasure."

The song "Smoke Gets in Your Eyes", performed by Gertrude Niesen, started to play and Walter and Dorothy swirled and glided around the room, staring raptly into each other's eyes. I hadn't previously heard this version of the song as the Nat King Cole one was more popular, but I cherished hearing another version because I've always loved the song.

As they whirled across the floor, Walter seemed to be lovingly crooning the lyrics to Dorothy. He broke off, nuzzling Dorothy's hair with his nose and bringing his mouth down to Dorothy's for a kiss that melted my heart. As they kissed, he raised his right hand up to the side of her face to gently caress his thumb across her cheek. I involuntarily sighed at how in love and enchanted with each other they seemed to be.

I loved seeing them together and glanced over at Ryan, who was looking steadily at the door instead of the couple as if he felt he was intruding on a secret moment. Which, okay, sure. We totally were, but it's not like Walter and Dorothy had any indication we were watching them from the future.

Pulling apart from their embrace, Walter brought Dorothy over to the loveseat in the office. When seated, he took her left hand in both of his and coughed, seemingly nervous when he had seemed so confident just moments ago in their dance.

"Dorothy, you know how much I care about you," said Walter. "You have made me the happiest I've ever been and I can only hope that I've brought even just half the happiness to you that you have to me."

"Oh, Walter," grinned Dorothy swatting him on the shoulder with her free right hand. "You know that you have, you silly goose! What on earth has brought this on?"

"I know that I'm not following the correct protocol here," said Walter, as he stood up and then leaned one knee on the ground, bringing about a gasp from Dorothy. "I can't afford a ring for you at the moment, nor have I asked your father for your hand. But, I know that I love you and do not want to waste another moment more without you. So, I hope you will grant me the privilege of becoming my bride. Will you marry me, Dorothy?"

Dorothy whooped with joy, jumped up, and threw her arms around Walter's neck, murmuring "Yes, yes, yes!" in between kisses. She broke free from kissing Walter only to say, "I love you, too, Walter! So very much!"

The pair continued their celebratory make out session, wrapped in each other's arms, as they fell onto the loveseat with Walter on top of Dorothy in a very heated embrace. I started to blush watching them.

Just as Walter begin to run his hand up underneath Dorothy's skirt, the room thankfully spared us the rest of the scene and started spinning again.

CHAPTER 17

"Oh, my gosh," I said as the room stopped swaying. "Thank you, thank you, thank you, ghosts or whoever for not letting us see the rest of that!"

"I don't know about that," grinned Ryan. "Dammit. It looked like it was just about to get really good."

"Ha!," I chuckled. "And here I thought you weren't looking at all! Stop that, you! Let them have their privacy back in the 1930s or 1940s, whenever that was."

Thinking for a minute, I continued, "I'm confused, though. If they were so happily engaged as they certainly were there, why didn't Emma wind up marrying Walter and instead told her mother she'd marry Raymond. And how did Raymond not know about the baby?"

"Huh," pondered Ryan. "About that baby... I wonder if what we would have witnessed there was the conception..."

"Ack!", I said sticking my fingers in my ears. "La la la! Okay, I don't know why the thought of that grosses me out because it's not like sex is something horrid, but the thought of seeing their baby conceived is just skeeving me out to no end. Okay, another topic, please!"

"How about we talk football and the Pats?," joked Ryan.

"Nice try," I laughed. "Hmm, I hope that Dorothy remembered to pick up those tulips she brought in and put them in a vase. They were so gorgeous and how sweet that Walter picked them for her from the garden even though he wasn't supposed to."

"Women and their flowers," said Ryan. "How is it that just a simple bouquet of flowers can make a girl so freaking happy?"

"Oh, no, no, no," I said. "It's not just any bouquet of any flowers. For me, it has to be tulips or nothing because I just can't stand roses. Seriously. It's partially because of the totally overplayed roses on 'The Bachelor' and also it's such a stereotype for guys to bring roses when they're apologizing for something they did. Just screams overkill and like 'I'm sorry, baby. Ike'll never do it again!' only for them to turn around and do whatever they did over and over again. Drives me insane. But tulips. Those are different. Ohhhh, they just signify springtime, joy, happiness, and love to me. Nothing else will do. Aww, I wish I had a bouquet of them in my hand right now."

I looked down where a bouquet should have been, realizing I still held the fountain pen in my hand. I tried to write on a piece of paper with it to see how it worked for novelty's sake, but the ink had dried out years prior. Dropping it back onto the table and turning my attention to the papers there, I didn't realize that the pen kept going and rolled right off the desk onto the floor.

Leaving the futility of the door behind him, Ryan walked over to the desk as he saw the pen drop and bent down to pick it up. While he was leaning over to get the pen, he noticed an envelope on the floor peeking out between the desk and the little couch next to it. Picking it up, he said, "Actually, I wonder if Emma used this office as her own for correspondence instead of Edward at one time, since this envelope is addressed to her."

I took the envelope from him and turned it over, noting that it was open. Taking out a sheet of paper and a black and white photo, I first looked at the letter, reading to Ryan, "Mrs. Adamson, I am delighted to inform you that William has been placed with a fine family and is quite healthy and happy. I have enclosed a photograph of him for you to see for yourself in case you ever want to share it with your family down the road. I have inquired with the family about the possibility of giving you their name and will be in touch with it if they are amenable to the idea. Dutifully yours, Mister Richard Wingham."

Turning over the photo with surprisingly shaking hands, I found a photo of a chunky baby boy smiling for the camera. He had light hair and a winning grin that seemed vaguely familiar. I was touched by how cute baby William was and couldn't help but grin back at the photo, which was silly because it's not like he could see me.

"Oh, how happy and sweet," I crooned. "It looks like he really did wind up with a family that cared for him. I'm still sad for Dorothy, though, that she wasn't able to know about nor see William for herself and raise him. I wonder if Emma ever did give in and tell Dorothy about her baby's fate."

"It's interesting that Emma even kept this letter and photo," said Ryan. "You'd think that she would have burned it upon receipt to make sure no one ever found it."

"Maybe she meant to, but forgot," I said. "Although, I can't think of what would have made her forget about this photo -- considering it's a picture of her grandson."

"Well, there was the deadly wedding reception here," Ryan reminded me. "If this photo had arrived shortly before that, the events of that reception could have easily caused Emma to forget about the photo, and then it wound up brushed aside on the floor underneath this couch."

"That makes sense," I said, and then realized something I hadn't yet considered about that reception. "Oh, my God! That deadly wedding reception that occurred here -- it was probably Dorothy and Raymond's wedding. They must have been the couple that died. How didn't that light dawn before now? Oh, I so hope Dorothy didn't die not knowing that her son was actually alive nor be reunited with him. How dreadful!"

"Sadly, that would account for Emma not coming back into the office to find and burn the letter," said Ryan. "If she was mourning the loss of her daughter after such an awful event, the photo might have become a forgotten memory. Plus, she wouldn't have to worry about hiding the news about William from Dorothy anymore, so it wouldn't be at top of mind."

Tearing up, I said, "Poor Dorothy and poor William. A parent and child shouldn't be torn apart like that without any chance to be with each other and know each other. I feel just awful for them!," I sniffled, feeling like an ass for tearing up.

"Ugh!", I said. "What the hell. I shouldn't be crying over a picture of a baby I don't know. I think this is just getting to me because my parents died in a car accident and I never got a chance to say goodbye to them. They were in that car because they were coming to pick me up for my college graduation dinner. If I'd just gone straight to dinner with them instead of being a selfish tool and wanting to spend more time with my friends, they'd still be alive."

I broke into sobs, hating myself for being so emotional over a picture.

"Oh, you poor thing," said Ryan, pulling me to him for a hug. "No wonder you don't want to think about Dorothy and William not knowing each other when you've lost your parents. I'm so sorry for your loss. Just remember, though, that you did know your parents and got the chance to love them. Obviously, I never met them, but I can tell just by knowing you that they were awesome because your parents helped to make you the caring person you are today. I'm sure they really loved you and you them."

His kind, sweet words and the fact that he was listening to me and taking my thoughts into account instead of glossing over my feelings and paying no heed to them caused me to cry even harder and I buried my head into his shoulder, guiltily relishing the feel of those quite strong arms around me at the same time. Ryan patted my back and kissed the top of my head soothingly saying "There, there. It's okay, Maura. Cry it out. It's okay."

I pulled back just a little bit and looked up at him, while still clinging to him. "I'm so sorry, Ryan. I haven't cried this hard over my parents passing in so long. I thought I was all cried out over them, but I guess not."

"Shh," he said, lightly brushing my forehead with his lips and wiping away a tear from my cheek with his thumb. "It's okay. I'm here for you, Maura. You're going to be okay. I promise you that."

Ryan started humming a song I didn't recognize at first and then moved his right hand to the back of my waist and took my right hand in his left to dance with me to give me something else to focus on.

Lost in the moment, I moved along with him to the music he was creating, savoring just how right it felt to be dancing with Ryan from his height (my head nestled just perfectly into the crook of his neck) to how confident he was dancing and leading me around the room.

We continued to dance across the red and gold Persian rug in the library and it was like being in a dream, or as if I had stepped into the dance scene from "Beauty and the Beast", although Ryan was certainly no Beast. I was in a library, surrounded by a gazillion books, and being held by the man of my dreams, who I was beginning to realize with shock was humming "Smoke Gets In Your Eyes". Huh. Guess that little scene from the past that we'd encountered had stayed with him, too. I glanced to the side to see if the Victrola was still there, and sure enough it was, but it wasn't playing.

As I started singing the words of the song, I felt Ryan smell the top of my hair, which threw me off for a moment as I oddly tried to remember what shampoo I'd used that morning that could be so interesting.

"Mmm, your hair smells like lush flowers," said Ryan. "I had no idea."

"Wait. What the hell? Flowers?", I thought. "My hair should smell like mint, if anything, from my peppermint-scented shampoo, but really, it should smell like just a hint of the hairspray I dashed over it this morning, and that's not floral."

I was about to ask Ryan why he said that when the scent of tulips hit me, although I had no idea where it was coming from. It certainly wasn't my perfume (which had more of a musky scent to it) nor my hair. It was so overpowering that it seemed to envelop us and I felt intoxicated and swept away by the aroma.

Ryan nuzzled my hair with his nose and brought me closer to him as if to get closer to the enchanting scent. His lips brushed across my forehead and nose and then found my eagerly waiting lips. I felt a jolt of lust shoot through my whole body as his lips met mine and he clearly felt the same as we hungrily kissed each other like teenagers, tightening our embrace to get even closer to each other.

Somehow, we moved away from the desk and over to the sofa. Ryan tore my cardigan off before setting me back against the cushions to run his hands and then lips and teeth lightly over my now bare shoulders and neck, which arched in response. I clung to his back and ran my hands up underneath his shirt, relishing in the feeling of his strong back muscles and his body against mine.

I'd wanted this to happen for so long and couldn't believe how much better reality was versus when Ryan and I were together in my dreams and fantasies. Feeling quite weak in the knees, I was grateful that we weren't standing up as we continued kissing each other hungrily.

I'd never felt this turned on before ever and that was certainly saying something, considering the time I'd spent with Spencer, who was like a blonde Greek god. It was like I was in a drugged haze, acting without meaning to. And lord, this was no time to think about Spencer! My tank top was pulled halfway up and I had my hand on the button of Ryan's pants when a loud crash came from right above our heads upstairs.

Startled, we jumped apart and up onto our feet from the sofa. The smell of tulips vanished as we stood and instantly, I felt like I'd regained my senses. I could only assume that the same had happened to Ryan as he looked a bit shell-shocked. I grabbed my cardigan from the floor and we pulled our clothes back together to head upstairs, presuming that the noise was Kitty and Travis having found a way out of this damn house. As we ran, the reality of what had just occurred in the library came flooding back and filled my brain along with regret and guilt.

CHAPTER 18

When the guilt hit me, I stopped short at the bottom of the grand staircase gasping. "Oh, my god, Ryan," I started rambling from nerves. "What did we just do? That wasn't like me at all! Ugh, that should never have happened. I mean, holy shit. You're engaged, and to my boss no less! I'm such an asshole. I know. I know. You're just lonely because she's away, so that's why you kissed me. That has to be it. It's the only explanation for what just happened. I shouldn't have kissed you back, let alone the rest of it. Oh, crap. She's going to fire me. But I love my job. And I'm rambling. I know I am. I'm an awful, awful person!"

"Maura, honey, it's okay," Ryan said. "I didn't expect that to happen at all. Not even remotely, actually. I'm just as surprised by it as you are, but I promise Ashley won't fire you and I promise I didn't kiss you because I was feeling lonely."

"No, no, she will!," I said. "I'll have to tell her and then she'll fire me and it will be entirely warranted. And here I was so happy two seconds ago to know we were about to be out of this damnable house when we heard that noise."

"Seriously, Maura, she won't," said Ryan. "You have to trust me on that. Like I said, I'm shocked as you are that we started kissing because I'm not sure how that came about, but now that it happened, I'm not unhappy about it. Quite the opposite."

Despite our rush to find out what had happened upstairs and get out of the house, he stopped me from continuing up the stairs, took me gently by the shoulders and turned me to him.

"Ashley and I are no longer engaged," Ryan said, rendering me speechless. "Everything's fine. I'll tell you all about it, but long story short, we called off the wedding. However, Ashley didn't want to announce the broken engagement with the celebrity wedding plans going. She thought it would take away from the news of that wedding in the press or steal their thunder, so we will formally announce our news when she returns. Hell, she even had Kitty write up the press release so Ashley could approve it right before she left on her trip -- but didn't tell her the reason we split, so Kitty probably thinks I got cold feet or am just a jerk who called off the wedding to hound around."

"Ahhhh," I said. "Well, that certainly explains Kitty's statement on what she thinks are your quite charming feelings of love and marriage."

"Exactly," exhaled Ryan. "Ashley and I are both fine and still friends. We just aren't romantically compatible for the long term and that's okay. Better to figure this out now and not realize it until after the wedding when we both wind up feeling like we're just roommates. It probably also helps that Ashley has fallen in love with one of the film guys who is also working on the Kardashian wedding. That's another reason why I'm here instead of working there. It would be a bit awkward for me to be there with them. Hell, for all I know, they're eloping right now while they're in Europe and I would be thrilled for them if it happened."

"So, wait a minute," I said shyly, as I still couldn't believe what I was hearing. "This means you're single, unless you're already dating someone... Oh, god, please don't be dating someone. That would be just my timing and luck."

"Well," said Ryan sheepishly. "I'd say I'm single just until you agree to go out with me to dinner when we get out of here. I've always thought you were attractive and smart, but kind of figured you were very straight-laced and focused 110% on your job without a fun side at all, minus those little glimpses I'd get here and there when we were all out. But, seeing you do that little dance in the hallway this morning damn near knocked me on my ass with just how happy, fun, and full of life you are. And I know you're kind-hearted. That's what I'm looking for in the next person I date -- someone I can just have a great time with no matter where we are or what we do and that I want to spend all of my free time with instead of apart. And, hell, if that kiss and the rest back there -- wherever it came from -- was a pretty solid indication of the future, then I think we have something pretty special already because that was hot."

He pulled me to him for a sweet kiss and my heart fluttered.

"Guess this means I have even more incentive to get the hell out of this house, hmm?," I said, trying to rein in all the thoughts running rampant in my head. Could Ryan actually really like me for me? Holy shit. I wanted to jump up and down and squeal with happiness, and this time I wouldn't care if Ryan saw it because the cause was him. "Let's go locate Kitty and Travis, see what that commotion was all about, and get out of here through the hole they shot through the glass door or whatever they did."

As we happily reached the landing at the top of the stairs, which continued up to both the left and right, we saw an ashen-faced Travis above us on the landing to the right. That knocked the happiness out of me with a single glance.

Walking up to him tentatively, I put my hand on his shoulder and softly asked, "Travis, where's Kitty? I thought you guys found a way out of here, but from the look on your face..."

He wouldn't speak, which was even more out of the norm for Travis than his actions from most of today and was quite concerning. All he did was point down the hall and then walk down to the bedroom in the corner and stop at the open door. Cold air hit me again, but I wasn't sure if it was the actual cold this time or just dread trickling down my back. I suddenly felt fearful and pretty certain that we weren't about to find a way out awaiting us in that room nor Kitty standing there with a big grin and hug. Ryan and I carefully stepped past Travis into the room and stopped in our tracks, gasping in horror at what we found. Kitty was lying face up on the rug, dead, with a bloody forehead and a large shard of glass sticking out from her neck.

CHAPTER 19

"What the hell happened?" I yelled, turning on Travis as he and Ryan tried in vain to keep me from rushing over to Kitty's side, probably fearing that I was going to try to pull the piece of glass out of her neck and wind up injuring myself in the process. I frantically checked for a pulse, but knew I wouldn't find one considering the amount of blood surrounding her as well as her unseeing open eyes, and sadly didn't.

"You guys were supposed to stay together up here during your search for a way out. If you'd been together, my best friend in this whole wide world would still be alive or it might have been you laying there with a piece of glass stuck in your neck instead of her. And to be blunt, right now that seems like a far better option to me so I'd have my best friend back. Where the fuck were you? Why didn't you save her?! How did this even happen?"

Finally finding his voice, Travis replied, "I was taking a look around the men's sitting room with Kitty testing the windows, but then I got distracted by looking at some papers in a drawer. I wanted to see if there was anything important in them when Kitty wandered off to check out the other rooms. I told her not to go and to wait for me, but she wouldn't listen and she mentioned something about a glass door leading onto a balcony that she had seen in passing. It was behind that armoire over there, so she must have been trying to move it and tripped and fell into the mirror next to it, which broke. As the glass broke, one of the jagged pieces must have flown out and hit her in the neck at just the wrong angle."

"That doesn't make any sense," I said. "Kitty wouldn't have tried to move a freaking armoire on her own. She's stronger than she looks, but she's not that strong. That armoire has to weigh about 150 to 200 pounds. And besides, even if she had, I don't see how she could have been trying to move it and then fall with enough force to shatter the mirror when she hit her head on it let alone wind up with that freaking shard in her neck. She's not stupid! You didn't hear her call you to help her push it?"

"Beats me," said Travis. "I came in here after I heard the glass break and she was on her side on the ground. I thought she'd just tripped and broken the mirror on her way down, so I went over to her and rolled her over to help her up and brush the glass off her hair and that's when I saw all the blood and that piece of glass. By the way, took you guys long enough to get up here! Where the hell were you?"

The thought ran through my head that if we had come upstairs right after we heard the noise instead of stopping for that conversation on the stairs, Kitty might still be alive. But I had to stop that line of thought because it wouldn't do any good and Kitty was probably killed instantly when the glass entered her jugular. Ugh. What was I going to do without her? My previous joy had changed quite quickly to sorrow.

Thankfully, Ryan replied to Travis because I was at a loss for a response, saying "The door to the hallway from the library got jammed -- thought for a minute we were stuck in there, too. But I was able to get us out, and we stopped for a moment on the stairs to talk about that stuck door and how weird this place is."

Before Travis could ask any other questions about our delay, Ryan quickly changed the subject to the room we were in as he looked around. "Hey, let's take a look at that door to the balcony. Maybe there's a way off the balcony to the ground without say jumping off and breaking any bones -- like a ladder or stairs or something -- if we can get this door or the nearby window open."

Ryan and Travis worked together to push the armoire very gently at my insistence away from the balcony door so it wouldn't fall on Kitty. Yes, I knew it wouldn't injure her any further, but still. That was the last thing I wanted to see. I wouldn't have been able to handle having it crush her as I was already traumatized by seeing my best friend dead.

After the armoire was moved away, we went over to the balcony door and were not in the least bit shocked to find that it wouldn't open. Glancing out through the glass, I watched a bird perched on the ledge of the balcony look at us and then fly away. "Man, I wish I was that bird," I said wistfully. "It can come and go from here whenever it wants."

Semi-jokingly, I turned to Ryan and said, "NOW can I take Kitty's stiletto and break the glass on that door?"

"You certainly can," Ryan replied, "but unfortunately it won't do any good because I don't see any way off that balcony that doesn't involve jumping. If it was snowing and there were piles of snow out there to softly land in, I'd try, but since that's just hard ground out there, I wouldn't risk it."

Moving away from gazing longingly out the window at the outside, I took a look at the bedroom we were in. Dark pink roses adorned the wallpaper and the bedding was a dusty rose coverlet. Taking that coverlet off the bed to respectfully cover Kitty's body after shutting her eyelids, I said "This was either Dorothy or Elizabeth's room. They mentioned it on the tour, but I was only half-listening then because I was so excited about having the event here."

"Yeah, that makes sense," said Travis. "I'd bet it was Dorothy's room and she's a vengeful spirit in this house because she's the one who lost her baby and then had to marry that guy, even though I don't get why she's angry about that since he seems like he was a much better choice than the other guy by far. I mean, come on. He was wealthy and could give Dorothy everything she wanted. Why wouldn't she choose him over that little peasant? So, yeah, if someone were to die in the house at her hands, I can see that it would be here where Dorothy's spirit thinks her baby died. Dorothy's ghost probably grabbed Kitty and threw her into that mirror."

"But why?," I asked, not really expecting an answer. "Kitty was the sweetest person in the world and she'd never hurt a soul. Anyone should be able to see that at a glance, including a ghost. Plus, she has nothing to do with this house. It's not like she caused Dorothy's death. She certainly didn't deserve to die. None of us do, and by the way, how the hell could a spirit push her into a mirror? We haven't encountered the spirits moving anything -- just them being there for us to view. This makes no sense at all. Ugh. I just don't understand this and I don't think I'm going to anytime soon."

Looking down at Kitty's body underneath the coverlet, I sniffled and said, "Can you guys give me a few minutes with Kitty to say goodbye, please?"

Ryan and Travis went out into the hallway and respectfully closed the door halfway to give me some semblance of privacy, but to also leave the door a bit open in case anything else happened in the room, considering what had happened to Kitty. Hopefully, it wouldn't because I still didn't believe a ghost caused her death, but better safe than sorry.

I went over to Kitty and it finally and fully hit me that she was gone. I laid down on the ground next to my best bud and kissed the coverlet over her forehead, careful not to accidentally jab myself with the piece of glass now protruding through the coverlet. I felt tears come on as I realized that I'd never again hear Kitty's infectious laugh that could always brighten my spirits; grab a latte with her; be able to call her at any time of the day or night to talk, knowing she'd be there and I'd likewise be there for her calls; nor see her up on the stage where she was at her best singing and dancing her heart out for the world one more time. They say that a person's life flashes before their eyes as they die, but now it was Kitty's life that was spinning circles through my brain. She was the epitome of the term "full of life" and now she was dead. How was that fair?

"Don't leave me!," I wailed. "Oh, Kitty, please come back! Life won't be the same for me without you in it. I so don't want to believe that you're gone and that I'm never going to see you again. What am I going to do without you? Who am I going to talk or text to about all my malarkey? You were everything to me and seriously made me who I am today. I will never forget you for that. Because of you, I found strength I didn't know I had and I hope that I'm not going to lose that strength without you here to remind me of it. Hell, I'm going to need every ounce of that strength and then some just to keep going without you beside me. I love you so much, my dearest friend. Please, please, please don't leave me. Come back!"

My thoughts of having Kitty taken away from me so abruptly turned my sadness to anger momentarily and I yelled out, "By the way, to whoever did this, if you're here and listening, mark my words that you're going to fucking pay for it! I swear! If it is you, Dorothy, I'm going to go all Ghostbusters on your dead ghostly ass, despite how bad I felt for you just a few minutes ago when I was thinking about you, Walter, and William not being together. And, if the person who killed my friend isn't a spirit, and you're nearby and can hear me, you better get the hell out of this house before I find you because I will tear you limb from limb, you despicable, murderous bastard."

With that out, I took a deep cleansing breath and calmed down enough to continue giving Kitty a proper private heartfelt goodbye. "Godspeed, my good friend. Thank you so much for being the wonderful you that you are - - dammit, you were. That one's going to take a while because I don't want to think about you not being here. I really don't. Can't imagine it. You helped me to find, embrace, and let out my weird and goofy side and loved me all the more for that part of me. I always thought that if I dared to show who I really was and how I really felt, people would run from me and that I needed to squelch anything that wasn't the norm, but you showed me otherwise and thank god for that."

Sobbing without care now, I continued, "You seriously were my soul sister and I loved you so freaking much. I hope you knew just how much you mattered to me. You really did help to bring me out of my shell and actually live my life and I am forever grateful to you for that. Although, who is going to make me sing karaoke up on stage now? Okay, fine, I'll do so in your honor, but I'll be wishing you were up there with me, and it's not going to be for a while because otherwise I'll burst into tears thinking about you while singing. Dammit, I'm going to miss you and never, ever forget you and I really don't know what the hell I'm going to do without you here." I desperately wanted to hug my friend one more time, but didn't want to move the glass shard in her neck and cause a bloody geyser. Despondent, I fell to the floor besides Kitty's body with my arm across her waist to be at least somewhat close to her one last time and sobbed for what felt like an eternity, but was probably only a few minutes in reality.

CHAPTER 20

Feeling a hand on my shoulder, I looked up at Ryan, who was gazing at me sympathetically. "Come on, Maura", he said giving me his hand to help me up. "Let's check out the windows in the other rooms up here and also see what's in that sitting room because Travis is chomping at the bit to get back in there."

Leaving the room, we looked into the small room/closet that was in between that bedroom and another one. The stark room contained just rods and hooks where clothing and linens used to be, and no windows, so we only stayed in that room briefly.

The next bedroom was in a very pale shade of pink, which would make it Elizabeth's bedroom if the first one was indeed Dorothy's as Travis suspected. This room was lavishly decorated and featured two large windows. Neither one opened, to no one's surprise at all. I think by this point if any of the windows had opened, we would have let go of them in shock, and they would have shut back down and not reopened.

As we made our way through the other bedrooms on the floor, plus the bathrooms and closets for each, we hazarded a guess at who had lived in each room.

Two of the bedrooms were decidedly the boys' rooms as they featured shades of deep blues and greens. One of the brothers -- either Stephen or Henry -- must have had a strong affinity for boating, as the blue room featured mariner charts decorating the walls. There was also a sextant and compass prominently displayed on the teak desk in the room to complete the look.

Sports were highlighted in the green bedroom, with a baseball sitting under a glass case on the dresser. A worn football lay resting on top of the bed like it had been casually thrown there by the boy as he came into the room and hadn't been moved since. I wondered if that actually was the case or if it had just been set that way by Wilford and the housecleaners to appear so for tours to give the room more of a personal feeling. Considering the room was so clean and didn't contain a speck of dust, I suspected the latter.

The last bedroom on the floor must have been the master suite. It was the largest bedroom and seemed to be decked in gold, from the gilt paneled walls to the light gold bedcover and pillow shams, the gilded chandelier to the ivory and gold chaise; and even the gold, ivory and white oriental rug on the floor. Light gold curtains covered the windows. Unfortunately, pushing them aside led to the same discovery as the other rooms -- windows that refused to open.

Feeling morose as we left the master bedroom and neared the sitting room, which was the last room on the floor, I sighed. "Are we ever going to get out of this house? Someone will have to show up eventually, right? Like the construction team; the caterer; Wilford; or the guests for the Winter Dance later tonight. But, ugh, that's not for hours. What's going to happen to us between now and then if we don't find a way out?"

Even though we were in a large, roomy house, I suddenly felt quite nauseous and claustrophobic. This was different than the feeling I'd had before the psychic memories displayed in the house. I felt trapped and scared along with feeling like I was going to be sick. I leaned my head against the wall to try to ease that feeling with the coolness of the wallpaper, figuring it had worked other times in the past when I was feeling off.

When that didn't help, I ran past Ryan and Travis into the sitting room and straight over to one of the windows looking onto the front lawn, feeling suddenly even more desperate than ever to get out.

"Why is this house trying to keep me locked in here? Let me out! I don't belong here!"

Great. Now I have Radiohead's song, "Creep" (or "Creek" as we called it back in school – queen of misheard lyrics here, folks. When I sing it, the lyrics are "I'm a creek. I'm a river...") stuck in my head.

Stop it! That's not helping... Okay, I need to concentrate. Come on. Think. I need to find a way out to get help. Can that window open?

Nope. Of course it doesn't. That would be too easy. Grrr...

"Dammit! Let me out of here! I don't want to die!"

CHAPTER 21

Seeing that I was quite a bit on edge (understatement of the century), Ryan came over to me and enveloped me in his arms, patting my back, kissing my hair and telling me in a soothing voice that we would find a way out, and that we would be together and have that dinner he'd promised.

"Hmm, now isn't this an interesting development," snickered Travis in a tone I'd never heard from him before, standing in the doorway and once again oddly stroking a mustache he didn't have. "I turn my back for one minute and look what happens. I'm disappointed though, Maura, since I thought you never dated coworkers. Guess you're just a lying little whore. Should I leave you two alone so you can go find one of those bedrooms and roll around in the sheets? You sure don't seem all that distraught. Maybe you can go get it on in the bedroom where your dead friend is. Boy, will Ashley love hearing about this. I can't wait to give her a call once I have cell reception again. Dammit, I should have gotten that on video as additional proof. She'll fire your homewrecker ass on the spot, Maura, if she doesn't rip you into shreds first."

"No, she won't," said Ryan, turning around to face Travis. "First, don't ever talk to Maura like that again. I thought you were better than that. As for the relationship I had with Ashley, we realized months ago that the reason we got engaged was that it just seemed like the next thing to do after dating for a while. But there was a big part missing -- we didn't love each other nor want to spend all of our days together. Hell, we even kept putting off moving in together because we both still wanted our own space. That kind of said a lot right there. Of course, we care for each other, but not enough to get married. And since neither of us really wanted to get married, the wedding kept being delayed and delayed. We finally had a chance to talk and when we admitted that we didn't actually want to marry each other, we were both so relieved it was ridiculous. So we ended it rather than continue on with our farce of an engagement. "

"That's right, Travis," I said, stepping out of Ryan's embrace, even though I wanted nothing more than to stay in his arms. "You don't know what you're talking about. Their engagement was over a few months ago and Ashley's happily dating someone else already. Now leave it alone and let us be happy, too, once we're out of here."

I didn't really want to add on information about Ryan and Ashley's broken engagement and her new relationship, but Travis had left me with no choice and Ryan had stood up for me previously and then again just now by telling Travis the truth, so it was time for me to do the same. Plus, I'd have done anything to wipe that freaking malicious smirk off Travis's face.

Ryan seemed completely at ease with Travis knowing everything, which was a relief. Considering the conversation closed, he ignored Travis and walked over to look through some papers that were sitting on a table next to one of the couches in front of the fireplace. I joined him and picked up the paper on top. Glancing at it, I saw a document with the name "William" on it. I gasped and almost missed what Travis said next, because that document sure had my attention from that name.

"Whatever," Travis said, cackling. "You should have just dated me and none of this would have happened. She's still going to can you, you little bitch, or just make your life miserable so you wind up quitting. And then with you gone and Kitty now finally also out of the way, I'll be her favorite planner. Okay, her only planner because all she needs is a man running the show anyway… And I'll get all of the events to produce. I win."

"What?!," I said, spinning around to face Travis, and putting down the paper, forgetting about it. "You just sounded like you're actually happy that Kitty is dead and almost like you caused that to happen. I sure hope that's not what you meant."

"Watch what you're saying, Travis," said Ryan. "Kitty just died and Maura was her best friend. Saying something like that in jest isn't helping matters.

And this time, I won't step in between you two if Maura goes to hit you for even implying that."

"Oh. Whatever will I do? Sir Galahad is here to come to the rescue of poor damsel in distress Maura from lil' ol' dastardly me," sneered Travis. "Please. You idiots really believed me when I said that Kitty fell into that mirror all on her own or was pushed by a ghost? You're more gullible than I thought! Give me a freaking break."

I was stuck dead in my tracks. Travis killed Kitty? Why?

I may not have been able to move because I was in shock, but Ryan sure could. He bolted over to Travis, who had left the doorway and was standing by the fireplace. Ryan went to grab Travis by the collar and was about to deck him when Travis sidestepped out of his grasp, bending down. Ryan reared his arm back for another hit, realizing too late that Travis had picked a wrought iron poker. Travis took advantage of the moment to slam the poker into the left side of Ryan's head.

"Ryan!!," I gasped. Seeing Travis take a step towards me with the bloody poker in his hand as Ryan slumped down to the floor, I ran out of the room racing for the stairs, hoping against hope that the house would be kind for once today and allow me to flee out those doors to safety and to get help for Ryan.

Taking the stairs two at a time in my haste, I prayed that I wouldn't be my usual klutzy self and tumble down. At least the fates were on my side there. Not daring to look behind me, I made it to the doors. Just as my hand reached the doorknob, I felt a hand close around my shoulder. Letting out a shriek, I tried to turn around to put up a fight or run, but the feeling of a gun against my back stopped me.

"Don't even think about it, Maura" said Travis. "I found this gun stuffed in the back of a drawer in that sitting room upstairs and now I'm glad I did because it's going to keep you from making even one wrong move against me. Turn around slowly with your hands up in the air."

Turning around, I looked at Travis's face, wondering how on earth I had once found him so attractive. The look on his face stopped me short because I could see the rage and anger coming from him. I could tell that he wanted me dead. How was I going to get out of this and save myself and Ryan?

CHAPTER 22

I searched Travis's face for even just a glimpse of the person I thought I knew. Knowing that he'd killed Kitty in cold blood, he now looked like the ugliest, most evil person in the world. Had I ever really known him? Thank God I hadn't accepted that date back when he first asked me out. Ugh.

"So, you're probably wondering what happened to Kitty, aren't you," said Travis. "Well, she didn't suffer… too much," he added mockingly to my absolute horror.

"First, let me go back to what was supposed to happen here," Travis said. "You don't know this, but I got here even earlier than you did, thanks to another set of keys from good ol' clueless Wilford. I had told him that you and I were dating and I wanted to get here early and surprise you with a proposal. He happily agreed to keep my secret. So I came into the house this morning and spray-painted those words in red on the wall behind the painting. Then, I figured that I'd bump into the painting at some point to make it fall and reveal the warning behind it. That way, you and Kitty would freak out and run out of the house since you're helpless little females. Neither of you would want to come back in the house since you're babies, so I'd step in and offer to take care of managing the Winter Event and wind up in Ashley's good graces and be her top planner from now on. Then, over time, she'd realize that a man would take better care of the business and she'd go stay home where she should be and I'd take over the business."

"What the hell are you talking about?", I asked. "You're talking like it's the olden days where men worked and women did nothing but stay home. That's not you, Travis! Even besides that, what about the door slamming and then not opening. Did you get someone to seal the doors and windows shut, too? And what about the people we've seen and the walls changing? Was that all some sort of weird hologram and you have lighting people hiding somewhere?"

"Nope, that wasn't me," said Travis pensively. "I wish it was because it was awesome and truly over the top. The door slamming shut was brilliant and I didn't even have to cause the painting to fall as it just fell on its own. Magnificent timing that. You should have seen the looks on your faces. You guys were so freaked. It was classic."

"You are horrible," I spat at Travis through clenched teeth. "So, why did you kill Kitty? She'd already made it clear she was never coming back to the house. You didn't have to kill her!"

"Oh, yes, I most certainly did," said Travis. "I was in the sitting room when Kitty found that window and balcony behind the armoire, but she didn't try to move it by herself. You're right. She knew she was far too much of a weakling to even attempt that. I did come into the room to help her. We were each going to stand on one side of the armoire and try to push it sideways -- Kitty was standing in front and I would be behind it against the wall using that for leverage. Well, as I went to walk behind the armoire, my shirt must have hiked up, so she saw the gun I'd found sticking out of the back of my jeans. I knew she was going to yell out, so I had to stop her. I butted her in the head with the gun and then slammed her into the mirror. It was just pure luck that the piece of glass flew out from the mirror into her jugular. So okay, she didn't exactly not suffer as she probably felt all of that, but hey, after that she died instantly."

"You bastard," I cried. "You're sick and twisted! And all of this over a job? What the hell were you thinking? Good lord, psycho! If you wanted to be promoted so much, there's this concept you could have looked into called doing a fantastic job and going above and beyond your job duties to be recognized for your hard work. Instead, you go and quite literally kill your competition! You are clinically insane!"

"Now, now, now. No need to be snarky. I prefer to think of it as being deeply committed to my career. Plus, I didn't officially kill her. The mirror did," smiled Travis, reaching to twirl a mustache he didn't have, which was a bit freaky. He even looked a bit surprised for a moment to not find hair there.

"You fucking delusional freak," I yelled. "The only reason I'm not wringing your neck right now is because of that damn gun. Ooh, what a big boy hiding behind a gun, and how do you know it's even loaded if you found it in a drawer, huh? It's not like I'm going to test that, but if you didn't have that, you'd be dead right now." I knew I was taunting a madman, but I couldn't help myself.

"Don't worry, sweetie," said Travis. "I'm sure you'll be wishing you were dead soon enough because there's no way you're getting out of here alive now that you know what I've done to both Kitty and your love, Ryan."

At the sound of Kitty and Ryan's names, fury enraged me. I yelped and tried to fling myself at Travis, reaching out for his neck with my hands to wring his neck after all. But, before I could get to him, or he could get to the gun, the room started feeling like it was spinning again.

CHAPTER 23

A musty smell hit my senses as the room stopped shifting around. Travis also seemed quite dazed at the change, which was probably the only reason he hadn't grabbed his gun and shot me.

A knock came at the front door and an older thin man wearing a suit, who I assumed was the butler, went to answer it. He sported black hair slicked back with pomade, and a narrow yet strong nose with a straight long mustache underneath. Feeling the rush of warm, flowery air entering the house from outside as the door opened made me sigh. Standing at the door was Walter, who ran into the house frantically.

"Where's Dorothy?," he asked the older man. "Is she upstairs? I need to see her before this wedding. It's wrong. She shouldn't be marrying someone else. She should be marrying me. We were engaged! I love her, even though she ended our engagement and will not tell me why."

"Actually, the person Dorothy should have been marrying all along and is indeed marrying is me," said the older man. "Allow me to introduce myself, as I don't believe we've yet met. I'm Dorothy's fiancé, Raymond Carrion. And you... Well, you must be Walter Powers. Yes, I know all about you. Dorothy has never mentioned you, of course. Why would she? You're persona non grata to her, and please let me know if you need me to translate that, since I'm quite certain from looking at you that you never took Latin. But, yes I've heard about your pitiful little existence from her mother."

"Oh, well, isn't this the embarrassing situation," said Walter, looking abashed. "I'm sorry, sir. Actually, you know what. I take that back as I'm not sorry at all, especially after what you just said. Proper etiquette be damned. I do love Dorothy and I know she loves me. If she's here and she sees me, even you will have to admit that that's true at a single glance."

"Well, thankfully, Dorothy is not home right now," replied Raymond. "She's in town with her mother picking out her trousseau for our honeymoon. But, while you're here, why don't we step out of the foyer and into the ballroom to discuss this like two gentlemen. I'm sure you'll come to understand that Dorothy is marrying the man she truly loves. Also, that that man is me."

"And I'm the whack job," sneered Travis. "At least I'm not trying to convince you that you love me instead of Ryan. Good lord. This guy's even kookier than I am, but in a truly awesome way."

"Hush," I said, and then realized I was trying to shush the guy with the gun in his hand. Smart, Maura. Really smart. We followed Walter and Raymond into the ballroom.

The ballroom was in a far worse state than I'd last seen it. The marble flooring had all been torn up and the wall had holes in it covered by tarpaulin to make room for the new windows.

"Pardon the appearance," gloated Raymond. "We're redecorating here for our wedding of the century. Sorry that you won't be invited, but only the winner of Dorothy's hand in marriage gets to attend and that's me."

As we walked across the floor, I remembered Wilford telling me about the construction work that had been done to the ballroom. One piece of the floor had been more rotted than previously thought, which meant the construction team had to dig up quite a bit more of that part of the floor than they planned and added time onto the construction. That left one large hole in the floor with piles of rubble and construction equipment, including hammers and mallets, all around it. Now that most of the rubble had been removed from the hole, the hole could be filled, with the floor then covered over by the new parquet flooring.

"Watch where you're walking," joked Travis. "Wouldn't want you falling into that hole and being left for dead back in the 1940s and trapped under the parquet flooring today, now would we? Because you know I'd just leave you there, kiddo, and happily dance on the floor over your corpse."

Glancing nervously at the floor and feeling like I was about to gag at the thought, I stepped cautiously over to the wall where I could still hear and see Walter and Raymond but not risk taking a costly misstep. Travis, of course, came right over to stand beside me and showed me his gun again as if to remind me to not make any sudden moves.

"So, what is there to discuss?," asked Walter. "I love Dorothy; she loves me; this wedding has to stop; and you can find someone else to marry. Does that all sound about right to you?"

"Hardly," said Raymond. "Sure, I may not love Dorothy, but I'm quite fond of her and she'll grow to be fond of me. Plus, I have money — far more money than you could ever make — and I can help her family with the cost of this home so they can continue to live in it. As it is, I'm funding this construction work to ensure the ballroom is at its finest for our wedding reception."

"I may not have much money," said Walter, "but I have love and that's more important and what Dorothy actually needs."

"Oh, yes," laughed Raymond. "Your great, true, awe-inspiring love. It's the type of love people write songs about. I know all about that love and about that child it produced..."

"What?," gaped Walter. "What child? Dorothy never told me she was pregnant. Why on earth wouldn't she tell me? Bring me to my child right now."

"You have a son," taunted Raymond, "but Dorothy doesn't know it was a son nor that he lived. He was placed for adoption at birth and Dorothy's mother told Dorothy that he had died. But he lives. Emma told me because she wanted to ensure I was still alright with marrying Dorothy. I told her it was fine and that Dorothy's real children would be the ones she has with me. Your son's name is William, by the way."

"Oh, and Dorothy was going to tell you she was pregnant," continued Raymond. "But when she went off to find you to tell you at the town fair, I arrived ahead of her and paid off that little trollop to go up and grab you and kiss you right as Dorothy came up behind you. She sure made it look convincing enough that Dorothy thought you were a cad and wanted nothing further to do with you."

"You scoundrel," shouted Walter, not caring who heard at this point. "So, that's why Dorothy called off our engagement by post instead of talking to me in person and has refused to see me since. What did Dorothy or I ever do to you to deserve that kind of treatment?"

"Oh, my dear sir," grinned Raymond. "This has nothing to do with you personally at all. I just know a good house when I see it and the only way for me to gain possession of this property down the road is for me to wed Dorothy. Once she's my bride, the house becomes mine by default. Why do you think I'm putting money into it?"

"So, you really don't care for Dorothy," yelled Walter. "Believe me, if you loved her even at all, you never would have kept the news of our son from her. You bastard!"

Walter shoved Raymond, who fell to the ground. Struggling to his feet, Raymond got up, pulling out a gun he had tucked in the back of his pants (I wondered if it was the same one Travis was now holding), and struck Walter over the head with it. Instead of falling to the ground, though, Walter stumbled and fell into the hole, further bashing his head on the rubble as he landed.

"Well," said Raymond, twirling the corner of his mustache and replacing the gun, "that will take care of that pesky problem. I know that I saw chlorinated lime in the gardener's shed, so I'll go grab that and use it to keep your body from creating a stench under the floor. And now this wedding preparation can continue without further interruption." He threw more pieces of rubble into the hole so that Walter's body would be covered and not seen, before he came back.

Brushing off the rubble and dust from his pant legs and lapels, Raymond turned to walk out of the room, causing the room to shift back into its regular form.

CHAPTER 24

"I sure do like that Raymond guy," chuckled Travis, again absent-mindedly twirling a mustache that didn't exist. "And here I was joking about you falling into that hole back then, but he sure wasn't. Hmmm, dude's got the right idea. I wish there was a hole in this floor now so I could just toss you in and call it a day. It would be an easy way to get rid of you. Do you see a sledgehammer around at all? Maybe some lime, too? I could create a hole. Presto. Poof. Annoying little twit be gone."

"You are disgusting and I'm beginning to think Raymond's ghost is messing with you or has possessed you considering the way you keep playing with your non-existent mustache like he does with his," I spat as I backed away, desperately hoping someone would arrive at the house to save me, but knowing how unlikely that was.

"Well, my dear," sneered Travis as he advanced closer to me, "that could indeed be the case. It would explain why I'm feeling like I have the power here. Oh, wait. That's because I'm the one with the gun! Although if I'm possessed, far better to be affected by Raymond rather than that weak little Walter."

I backed away, wondering if there was any way I was going to get out of this house now.

"Sure, try to get away," laughed Travis. "We're stuck in this house and there's nowhere you can go. Even if you go upstairs, I'll still find you. You could even lock yourself into a room, but oh, hey, look at that. I have a gun, so I could just shoot the lock. But I'll give you a little bit of a head start before I kill you. I think I like the chase."

As I turned to run, that now all-too-familiar nauseated feeling hit me. I groaned, wondering what we'd encounter next.

The ballroom was suddenly alit by candles; light streaming in from the windows; and the now glistening chandelier. A parquet floor gleamed under our feet and each table was covered with a white tablecloth, lush centerpieces, and plates of food. Travis and I found ourselves standing in between the reception tables, and I wondered briefly what would have happened to us if a reception table had been where we stood. Would it have manifested around us? Would we be cut in half?

I took my thoughts away from that trail and turned my attention back to the scene around us. In the corner, a standard white wedding cake covered with intricate lace detail and topped with a silver bell stood on a table waiting to be cut by the non-happy couple.

"Oh, hey, there's my boy!," said Travis as Dorothy and Raymond entered into their reception as their band, the Ink Spots, started playing "Night and Day" by Cole Porter. Raymond raised their clasped hands in triumph as they stepped into the ballroom, while Dorothy looked like she wanted to turn and flee. Why wasn't anyone noticing this?

Raymond escorted Dorothy through the tables and straight onto the dance floor, while the band moved onto their first dance song, which was their own popular tune, "I Don't Want to Set the World on Fire".

"Oh, no, no, no," I gasped. "This is their first dance, when the chandelier falls and kills them. I don't want to watch this, house!"

"Aww, and here I was just getting to like the guy," said Travis. "Now I have to watch my hero die. Well, hmm, this could be interesting. I wonder if I can interfere somehow and keep him alive. Just Raymond. I don't give a crap if Dorothy survives or not."

"Of course you don't," I said, "because you're an asshole and apparently a misogynist at that! But, hate to tell you -- that isn't how psychic energy works at all. If it was, we would have been out of this house a while ago. This is just like watching a movie. We can't interact with the past nor can they with us."

Watching the couple's first dance, I couldn't help but notice that Dorothy looked morose instead of blissful, while Raymond looked quite pleased with himself.

"Ugh, what a jackass. What would have been so wrong with Dorothy winding up with Walter instead of this gross lout?", I wondered out loud.

"The bad guy wouldn't have won if that were the case, and we can't have that, dearie," said Travis.

"Umm, in case you forgot," I said. "The bad guy didn't exactly win here. He died thanks to that chandelier above his head."

The chandelier sure appeared sturdy as I glanced up at it. How on earth did it fall? I walked closer to the couple, wanting to get a closer look at the chandelier in the past to see if I noticed anything.

Apparently, Travis had forgotten about his idea of giving me a head start to get away from him as he followed close behind me.

"I can't go anywhere, Travis," I sighed. "Remember where we are? Hello… Locked house, locked windows, you have a gun and are a psycho who wants to kill me, yadda yadda. I'm not trying to leave. I just want to get a better look at the chandelier."

"I know," said Travis. "I just want to be nearby in case there is somehow a way I can keep that chandelier from falling on my newfound buddy Raymond."

Rolling my eyes, I stepped closer to the couple. Dorothy certainly looked lovely in her pure white wedding gown, featuring a high neck, flouncy sleeves, a lace overlay and a bustled skirt, but each time she smiled, it didn't reach her eyes. None of the guests – nor Raymond for that matter – seemed to notice her true unhappiness, but I certainly did. Maybe because I had seen how she looked when she was truly happy as she'd been when I had seen her with Walter.

I kept my eyes peeled on the chandelier, hoping that I'd see whatever had caused the deadly accident so many years back.

As I gazed at the chandelier, I realized something was different and I was starting to see a spectral image come into view below it. "Holy shit," I said. "That's Walter."

"Hey," said Travis. "That's not fair. You're dead, dude. Go away. You lost. Now shoo."

Walter's ghost appeared standing behind Dorothy and Raymond, with his back to them. He seemed so confused, which made sense considering the last time he had been standing in that ballroom, he had been alive, and the room had also looked quite a bit different then. Glancing around, he took in the wedding scene in all its finery and then turned again, seeing the married couple for the first time. A look of horror and anger came over him as he realized that Dorothy had married the man who killed him, but that horror turned to misery when he saw the agony on Maura's face, and he realized that she had been forced into the marriage because he hadn't been able to tell her how he felt, about the misunderstood kiss, and to stop this wedding from happening.

He walked up to Maura and went to put his hand up to her face, but stopped at the last moment. I couldn't tell if he didn't want to touch her or realized that he couldn't. Whatever the reason, Walter took his hand away, seemed to steel himself, and walked away from the couple to stand at the wall, watching them.

Dorothy and Raymond danced for a while longer, with Raymond continuing to draw Dorothy to him and then spin her back out again and again.

"What is Walter doing?", I asked, really to myself, since I had no interest in speaking to the lunatic Travis. Glancing at Walter again, I noticed something I hadn't before. He was counting from each time Raymond spun Dorothy out to when he pulled her back to him, almost like he was timing it. Then, he looked up at the chandelier above their heads.

CHAPTER 25

"Nooo," I exclaimed. "He wouldn't! Why would Walter kill Dorothy? He loved her."

"Love's a funny thing, toots," sneered Travis. "See, I told you that I was the better choice than that guy. Oooh, now are you gonna say I'm possessed by Walter, too, since I killed Kitty and he sure looks like a killer to me."

"Shut up!", I yelled in frustration. "There's no way that happened. You didn't see Walter and Dorothy together. They were in love and you can't kill that kind of love. You just can't. I refuse to believe it."

"Oh, you poor, naive child," said Travis. "Well, I don't know about you, but I sure wish I had a comfy chair and some popcorn to munch on while we watch this play out and you get to see your boy, Walter, go all Manson on this adorable couple."

Walter continued to look between the chandelier and Raymond and Dorothy's dance. I wanted to turn my back in case Travis was even remotely right and Walter was so bereft that he killed Dorothy, but knew I needed to see for myself just what had happened in this room.

As Raymond pulled Dorothy back to him once more and prepared to spin her out again away from him, Walter leapt up into the air towards the chandelier, grabbing it with his hands.

"Holy shit!," Travis exclaimed. "Who knew ghosts could catch air like that? I don't even like the dude, but sign that boy up for the ghostly NBA!"

At first, Walter just hung from the chandelier and it swayed back and forth with him, but he continued moving, tugging on the arms of the chandelier with his hands like he was doing pull ups, fluctuating his gaze between where the chandelier met the ceiling and the couple below.

"How is he even getting that chandelier to move?," questioned Travis. "That shouldn't be possible. Dude's a ghost."

"No idea," I replied. "I mean I saw the movie 'Ghost' and in that movie, Patrick Swayze was able to focus his anger to make things move. This must be like the same thing here, since Walter sure has a lot of pent-up and warranted rage towards Raymond."

Walter continued his efforts and increased them even more so when Raymond spun Dorothy away. I realized that he was trying to topple the chandelier onto just Raymond while Dorothy was away from him, but knew where this was going and wanted to scream to get Walter to stop as it wouldn't work like he wanted.

Finally, Walter's efforts paid off for him and the chandelier separated from the ceiling and fell towards the ground.

Unfortunately for Walter, the timing was when Dorothy had just twirled back into Raymond's arms instead of when she was a bit away, so the chandelier crashed on top of their heads, knocking the couple down to the floor.

I wondered how none of the guests, nor the couple themselves, had even noticed that the chandelier was swaying, but decided it must have been that everyone was stuck in their own little world: Raymond feeling proud that he had "won"; Dorothy lost in her sadness of losing her baby and not having Walter stop the ceremony, which she was secretly hoping would be the case; and all of the guests lost in their own goings-on.

"Nooooo! Dorothy! What have I done?", moaned Walter, as the guests and family members swarmed screaming onto the dance floor.

The men at the reception all worked together to move the heavy chandelier up so they could get to Dorothy and Raymond to free them and hopefully find them just injured or bruised. As soon as the couple was free, though, it was clear that the damage had been done. Neither had a pulse and their crushed-in skulls and glassed-over eyes were further proof solid that they were dead.

A palpable hush of horror fell over the crowd. No one could believe that this had happened at a wedding reception that was supposed to be about love and joy.

Shortly, a scream broke the silence. "Dorothy!", sobbed Emma, running over to her daughter's body and grabbing her to her chest. "No! How did this happen? All I wanted was for you to be taken care of. This wasn't in that plan. Oh, my dear daughter! I'm so sorry. Forgive me. Forgive me. Forgive me!"

Edward was standing beside her and heard Emma's words. "What does Dorothy have to forgive you for, Emma?", he inquired.

Before a stricken Emma could reply, Edward gasped out loud and clutched his chest and fell to the floor. Emma let go of Dorothy and yelled for help.

CHAPTER 26

"Edward!," I yelled out. "He's having a heart attack! Oh, please let someone help him. He can't die the same day that his daughter did. How awful would that be?"

My first instinct was to go over and try to help him, forgetting briefly that I was watching the scene from another time and couldn't do a damn thing to change the past. As I ran, I saw and felt the room start to spin around me and stopped myself, remembering just where and when I was.

When we were fully back in the present, I hoped that Travis would be discombobulated enough that I could attempt an escape and maybe, just maybe I could get out.

I got as far as the entranceway to the ballroom when I was jolted backwards into the room by someone grabbing the back of my hair and yanking on it.

"Don't even try it, missy," sneered Travis, pointing the gun at my back, which felt all too familiar. "That ain't happening. You can't run off to your precious lover since I hate to break it to you, but he's dead. Now, we have a dance to do here and a happy crowd to greet."

"What the hell are you talking about? What dance? What crowd?", I said, but it seemed I was talking to a brick wall as Travis turned me around with one arm while holding the gun still in the small of my back. We walked back into the room as Travis steered me in a serpentine pattern through the room (was Travis somehow still seeing the tables that had been at the reception?) to the middle of the dance floor where Dorothy and Raymond had had their fatal first dance.

"Now then, my dear," said Travis, "put a smile on that face and be a good little wifey. It's time for our first dance as man and wife." He kept his right arm with his gun firmly at my back, put my left arm on his right shoulder, and then took my right hand in his left and lifted it up so that we were in a standard slow dance position. Without music playing -- that I could hear, anyway -- we started dancing across the floor.

"Oh, fuck," I thought. "Travis really IS possessed or psychotic. He thinks I'm Dorothy, he's Raymond, and this is our first dance. Marvelous. How am I ever going to get out of here now? And what is it with dancing in this house?"

I needed to figure out a way to appease him somehow without letting him think I was acting, so that maybe I had a chance of survival. Ugh! This was going to take the performance of a lifetime.

Painting the falsest smile ever on my face, I looked up at Travis and sweetly said, half choking back the words, "Look at all these guests here just for us, Raymond. They are all so very happy for us, aren't they? I'm such a lucky girl to be married to you."

"Well, that's more like it," Travis smiled. "That's my girl. You're finally coming around. I guess you've seen the light and realized you're much better off with me than that ridiculous yokel."

Leaning to whisper into my ear, Travis said, "You'll learn that truth even further about who's the better man when we're all alone tonight on our wedding night."

Even though Travis couldn't see my face as his was still close to my ear, I kept my face completely blank just in case. What happened next, though, further proved to me that Travis was gone and Raymond was the one in charge. He started to sing the lyrics of "I Don't Want to Set the World on Fire" to me, as if he was singing along with the band for Raymond and Dorothy's wedding reception.

Travis/Raymond's hand at my back tightened a bit more to pull me even closer to him. I wanted to break away, but knew that gun was still there, and feared it would go off if I made the wrong move. So, instead of leaning back, I fought every instinct I had and moved in even closer to Travis.

I slipped my right hand out of his and brought it up to drape along the back of his neck, running my fingers through the back of his hair and down his neck.

Travis's purr of delight showed me that he was getting distracted. I could only hope he'd let go of that gun -- and that the safety was still on, so it wouldn't go off, shooting me when he dropped it. Oh, I was putting a lot of faith into "what if's" here.

He was still singing along when I noticed something shimmer into view behind him and quickly dropped my hand back to Travis's shoulder, wondering what was going to happen next.

"Oh, please don't let it be Walter coming back to kill us, too, thinking we're Dorothy and Raymond!", I thought with horror.

As the image became sharper, I realized that it was instead Dorothy, still in her wedding gown. I wasn't sure what she could do to get me out of this situation, but seeing her gave me a spark of hope that there was still a chance.

She looked over at us, confused by our modern clothes to no surprise, and I mouthed "help" at her, not wanting to alert Travis to her presence.

Before I could get her attention, Travis twirled me away from him. Great, we were going to fully recreate Dorothy and Raymond's dance.

Thankfully, Travis didn't seem to notice Dorothy's ghost. Maybe only I could see her as I appeared to be connected to her based on what had happened in the library with Ryan.

As we twirled around again, she looked straight at me, and must have seen the gun before we spun around, as she held one hand up to her mouth in horror and reached her other hand out to me. I silently said "Help me! Please help me!" to her. Dorothy looked around for something she could do to intercede, but nothing struck her at first. Then, she looked up at the chandelier.

"No!," I screamed internally. "Not the chandelier, Dorothy. I don't want to die!"

CHAPTER 27

Since I knew what Dorothy was thinking about the chandelier and knocking it down, fear hit me and I frantically shook my head no in protest. I had seen all too well how that had worked out when Walter tried it. I wondered how Dorothy could even ponder it, considering what had happened to her.

Was there a shot that it would work this time and I wouldn't be killed as well? I also didn't want to really kill Travis because I could see that he had indeed been possessed by Raymond, but I wasn't sure if there was any other chance. If it came down to me living versus him, though, I'd choose myself.

I had to get him to drop that gun and just pray that the safety was on. But how?

"Oh, Dorothy, my dear," Travis crooned suggestively in my ear, "how I can't wait to get you alone and out of that dress. We are going to have quite a night together. Just you wait."

I grimaced, but knew what I had to do. "Oh, Raymond" I sighed. "Why can't we be alone together now? This dress is just so confining and I want nothing more than to take it off and be with you in every sense of the word. Please kiss me and give me something to tide me over til we're alone."

"Dorothy!", Travis gasped. "You little vixen. You have no idea how turned on I am right now."

I gazed up at him, feigning the most innocent, yet knowing look in my eyes. "Kiss me, Raymond", I demanded.

Travis pulled me even closer against him, dropping the gun. I flinched and gasped, waiting for the shot, but all I heard was the sound of the gun hitting the floor, thankfully. Raymond's spirit clearly took the gasp as a sign of lust, and pulled my face to him with both hands, devouring my lips hungrily with his.

Knowing what I had to do, I returned the passion in his kiss, but kept my eyes open (Travis' eyes were closed) so I could ensure Dorothy wasn't about to drop the chandelier on us.

"Oh, will this work with my wedding dress on and all the layers?", I thought, and then I came to my senses. "Holy hell, stop it. I'm not Dorothy and I'm not wearing a big poufy wedding dress. These are jeans, and that is perfect."

When I knew Travis was fully preoccupied with his tongue in my mouth, I reared my right leg back and threw my knee upwards and forward, striking him directly in the balls. Thankfully, it was a straight-on hit.

He grunted in agony, dropping to his knees and rolling over to his side. Quickly, I grabbed the gun and held it to him.

"If you get up and try to come at me again," I said, "I'm pulling the trigger, Travis. Yes, we were friends and you know how much I care about you, but I need to get out of this house and get help for Ryan and you are NOT going to stop me."

Off to the side, Dorothy pumped her fist into the air with glee, but that glee turned to horror when she and I saw Raymond's spirit shimmer half out of Travis's body to stand over him in fury.

"Get up, you coward!", yelled Raymond. "Shake this off and man up. Now go grab that gun from that girl and finish what you started and make her yours or kill her. Either way, get up off the ground!"

Before Raymond could taunt Travis further, Travis somehow roused himself enough out of the possession (maybe because Raymond's spirit wasn't fully in his body anymore?) to look directly at me. He was distraught and clearly said, "Dorothy, I know you don't want to, but shoot me. It's the only way to end this."

"No, Travis!", I said, "I can't do that. I just can't. Especially seeing that you're you right now. You can fight off Raymond. You have to."

CHAPTER 28

"Maura," Travis pleaded, "you have to. I'll be possessed by Raymond forever otherwise. Even if we got out of the house, he'd still be part of me, and he's fully intent on killing you. I can't let that happen, so please, kill me first."

I was still torn, but with those words, Dorothy leapt into the air towards the chandelier. She grabbed it and on the first try, it came crashing to the ground on top of Travis, crushing in the back of his skull, and nailing Raymond's spirit at the same time. I dropped to my knees in grief.

Raymond's spirit burst into flames, which gave me the briefest moment of satisfaction, as he couldn't continue to torture Dorothy in the afterlife. At least, I hoped that's what that meant. What wasn't as soothing was seeing Travis' spirit leaving his body, since I knew there was not even a chance of saving him now.

He saw me kneeling there, gasping in horror, and came over to me. "Maura, it's okay," said Travis. "I didn't want to die, of course, but I know that's what caused Raymond's spirit to be eliminated. That man was truly, truly evil. I could feel it inside me. I did get here earlier today because I was going to put a sign up of 'Congratulations, Maura!' on the wall so you'd see it when we came in. But the second I stepped foot in here, I could feel him taking over and was helpless to stop him from almost everything after that, including writing that on the wall behind the painting; pushing Kitty into the mirror, saying what he did, and bringing you down here and tormenting you like he did. I hope you know that of course I didn't do any of this on purpose, nor did I ever think that a woman's place is at home while the guy takes over. Holy old-school thinking! That was one scary mofo taking up space in my head. So glad he's gone. And yes, he is gone for good -- or at least he's down in Hell and not anywhere near Dorothy, Kitty, nor me, unless I'm going to Hell."

Travis looked devastated at the thought that his actions while being under Raymond's command could cause him eternal damnation. But he shook his head and continued. "Maura, there was a reason that Raymond wanted me to actually be married to you, besides the part of him that thought you were Dorothy. There's a piece of paper up in that sitting room that I uncovered in the back of a drawer when I was looking for that gun. It will change your life, I promise you"

"Travis, what are you talking about?," I asked. "Is that the piece of paper with William's name on it that I picked up before Raymond hit Ryan over the head? If so, I dropped it in the fray and have no idea where it is."

"You'll find it, "Travis promised. "I'm certain of it. You've been without family for so long and now you will have a family."

"I'll look for the paper when I go to check on Ryan, Travis," I said, standing up as a thought struck me. "But, speaking of family, what about your family? How on earth am I going to tell them?"

"Well, please don't tell them I was possessed, although they probably have thought and hoped I was for years anyway with all of my manwhore antics and that an exorcism would cure me," winked Travis, which brought tears to my eyes that the old joking Travis was back, only to lose him again.

"Oh, please don't cry, Maura. If anything, cry because you're never going to be able to date this hot ass. I kid. I kid. Plus, sistah, that was never going to happen anyway, since from the look of it, I think I'd be losing out to Ryan if he's okay up there -- which I hope he is because I think I was able to rally and grab the poker back a bit from Raymond's control so it just grazed him. I can't blame ya for wanting him. Dude is hot. He's no me, of course, but he's hot and you guys will be happy together."

Travis continued on, turning serious again, "As for my family, just tell them that it was an accident, since the chandelier has fallen here before, so there's precedence, and that you heard me say how much I love them before I passed away. That will help them, or confuse the heck out of them. Either way, they won't ask any further questions. I promise. And if you could also ask them to play 'Staying Alive' by the Bee Gees at the funeral, that would be great."

"You are such an ass, even dead," I laughed, through my tears. "And no way! Your folks would think I was terrible making a joke like that about your funeral!"

Something occurred to me that I had to ask Travis while I still could. "Why is it that I can see and speak to you, but I don't see Kitty's spirit around anywhere?"

Travis looked thoughtful for a second and said, "I'm no expert seeing as I've been not so much on the alive side for just a few minutes here, but I think it's because you were here when I died. Or it's because I needed to tell you something. You and Kitty have always had such a close friendship that I'm sure you didn't have any secrets from each other. That reminds me. When we're done talking, I need to go find her and make sure she knows that it was Raymond that caused her death and not me. I hope she understands that, because I'm going to need her friendship now more than ever."

"Please tell her I love her," I said. "If she was around, she heard me say all of that already after she died, but I'll feel better knowing you're going to tell her for me. And know that I love you, too. You really have been a great friend and I'm going to miss the shit out of you."

Travis lightly kissed my forehead in farewell, which I could shockingly feel, and said, "Now, listen to me on this one. Do this for me. Go embrace your life and live it as much as you can and then some. As our buddy Spike said during our 'Buffy' marathons with Kitty, 'You have to go on living, so one of us is living'. I love ya, and I'll be watching over you, though I'll try to make sure I'm not being a peeping Tom and checking in on any private moments. P.S. Don't forget about me, kiddo." Then, Travis' spirit vanished and I burst into tears. Far too much loss. I officially hated this day.

CHAPTER 29

I heard a cough, and turned, having forgotten that Dorothy was still there. She smiled and came over to me. "Thank you," said Dorothy, taking my hand. "Your bravery and actions have freed me from being stuck with Raymond in this house forever, which was like its own version of damnation."

She looked at me closer and continued, "My dear, may I ask your name? You look so familiar and I feel like I know you, but I can't have. Are we related?"

"Forgive me," I said. "I know your name and who you are so well that I forgot it's not the same for you. See, I feel like I know you from hearing about you and seeing scenes from the past..."

Dorothy looked beyond confused by that, so I decided it was better to skip over educating her about psychic energy and went on.

"Never mind all of that," I continued. "I can explain later if we have time. My name is Maura Hartwell."

"And your parents," Dorothy pressed on. "What are their names?"

"Were," I said sadly. "I lost them over 10 years ago from a car accident. My parents were named Sarah Lafferty and Mark Hartwell."

Dorothy looked stunned. "Lafferty? Oh, it couldn't be! Well, that could certainly explain it. If so, you've finally come home!" A smile lit up her own face.

"I'm sorry. What?", I said, startled. "Home? No, this isn't my home. It never has been. I live in Quincy. But why does the name Lafferty strike you?"

"William," said Dorothy, plainly. "Yes, I know about him. No, it's not like I learned something about him after I died while I was haunting the house. There's no way to do that, today being quite the contrary. I was in Mother's sitting room a few hours before my wedding lamenting that I had to marry Raymond and found a letter to my mother from a man named Richard Wingham saying that a baby named William had been adopted by Harold and Maude Lafferty. I confronted her and she admitted that my baby hadn't died at birth and instead she had put him up for adoption. Horrified, I ran off to tell Father, call off the wedding, and go find my love Walter and our son, but Mother located me in Father's sitting room before I could do any of that as Father wasn't there. She convinced me not to, saying that we needed Raymond's money as Father was more ill than I'd known. I was devastated, but hoped that once I was married, I could then go find the Laffertys and hope to at least meet my son, even if I couldn't reunite with Walter."

Glancing down with tears in her eyes, she sighed, saying, "Well, you know what happened next and what happened to Walter."

"Oh, my goodness," I exclaimed. "That's the document Travis was just telling me about, which I had found up in the sitting room. I saw William's name on it, but didn't have a chance to read further. And Harold and Maude Lafferty were the names of my great-grandparents, which means your son actually was my grandfather, and you're my biological great-grandmother. Oh, how did you know?"

"Blood knows blood," Dorothy said. "It's no wonder I felt so connected to you the second I saw you and wanted to protect you when I saw Raymond's spirit inside that poor man holding the gun. Have you felt even an inkling of the same?"

"Yes," I admitted. "I wondered why I was so emotional from seeing you in my glimpses into the past in the house, and well, it's no wonder now why I was a bit grossed out at the thought of possibly seeing you and Walter conceive William in the library…"

"You saw that?", yelped Dorothy. "Please tell me you didn't, because that IS where William was conceived, actually."

"No, no," I hurriedly said. "We didn't actually see the act itself, don't worry. It was just you and Walter collapsing onto the sofa and it was pretty clear what was going to happen next and then the scene disappeared."

"Oh, that's a relief!", said Dorothy. "That was certainly an act of love, but it was a private act, not meant for anyone else to see."

"I promise we didn't see a thing," I assured her. "And I want you to know that I did get a chance to know your son, William. He was a wonderful grandfather -- always so full of love and happiness and singing. He absolutely loved to sing to us. He passed away 15 years ago, before my parents passed on, but I remember every visit we had with him and my grandmother, his wife, Maggie. It was always such a fun time being with them and I never dreaded visiting them at all. They loved each other so much and raised my mother, Sarah, to be a truly magnificent, loving, and wise woman. Ohh, I miss them all every day."

I stopped, teary-eyed with joy at this semi-reunion, but sad that Dorothy would never to get meet William nor her granddaughter in person.

"Oh, my sweet child," Dorothy said, "don't cry. If you do, let them be happy tears for the time and years you had with all of them. I can only wish that I had had that time, but I'm so glad to hear that William was raised right in a clearly loving home and passed on that love."

"I don't have much time left with you," continued Dorothy, "but I need you to be brave, my dear, as you still need to get out of this house safely. I'm hopeful that now that Raymond is fully gone, that means that whatever is going on will have been lifted, but I can't promise that."

"I don't know if I can be brave," I confessed. "First, my best friend, Kitty, was killed; and Ryan was either killed or injured; and now my friend, Travis is gone. And my head is spinning. Since Raymond possessed Travis, I'm now wondering if your and Walter's spirits somehow affected us and that's why Ryan and I kissed and felt something for each other in this house. I can't imagine he would be interested in me otherwise."

"Oh, my dear," said Dorothy. "You are indeed brave. The woman I just saw here who got out of the situation she was in and who then proceeded to say goodbye to her deceased friend certainly had gumption and strength beyond her years. I don't know if you and Ryan were impacted by the love Walter and I felt for each other or if those feelings were already there and were just brought to the surface. That's up for you to find out."

"I'm scared," I admitted. "I don't want to go upstairs because if Ryan has died along with Kitty and Travis, I don't know what I'll do. But if he is alive, that brings along its own challenges of finding out the truth about our feelings and if they were real or just a mirage from the house."

"Be brave, my sweet girl," said Dorothy. "Trust your feelings and your intuition. That will give you more strength than you know."

With that, she shimmered away in a sparkle of light. I put my hand to my face, knowing that I had to go check on Ryan and try to get out of the house, but I needed a moment to process everything.

"Maura," said a voice from the hallway. "Maura, where are you? Are you okay?"

CHAPTER 30

"Ryan!", I yelled, running out of the ballroom. "Oh, my god, you're alive. Thank heavens. I'm here. I'm here!"

I found Ryan sitting on the bottom step of the grand staircase leaning against the bannister. He was holding a throw pillow to his head wound to staunch the bleeding and was also holding a piece of paper in his other hand.

"Maura," he said weakly. "Thank heavens you're okay. Where's Travis? Did he hurt you?"

I sat down next to him, and replied, "Oh, I'm fine. Really. It's a long story but Raymond possessed Travis, so that's why he was acting the way he did, said all those awful things, and why he attacked you. You would have been killed, but Travis was able to take over for a moment to deliver just a glancing blow with that poker and I'm so glad he did. He saved your life, Ryan! However, Raymond took back over and he wanted to kill me in the ballroom, but Dorothy appeared and she dropped the chandelier on Travis, which sent Raymond's spirit to Hell for good, but also killed Travis in the process. But I'm okay, I promise. Really. And oh, Ryan, you're alive! I can't believe it. I thought for sure you were gone... and I'm rambling again."

Ryan chuckled softly. "Okay, that was a lot to take in at once. How about we get out of this house and you can fill me in on it all then? I'm feeling quite weak, so you're going to have to help me up."

I put my arm around Ryan and helped him to his feet. We walked slowly over to the door and I gently propped Ryan up against my side so he wouldn't fall as I reached for the door handle, fearing the worst.

To my complete shock, it opened. "We're free!", I said. "Oh, Ryan, we're finally free of this freaking house!"

Ryan smiled weakly back at me. Once we got fully outside, I let him sit down on the outside steps and I ran to my car for my phone to call 9-1-1, quickly retrieving it from the backseat where I'd thrown it earlier that day.

As we waited for the ambulance to arrive, I also phoned Wilford to let him know in case he was home and saw the ambulance come rushing by as he lived in a cottage on the property by the main entrance.

Due to Wilford's proximity, he arrived with his wife, Elaine, before the ambulance. Wilford was wearing a red sweatshirt and jeans, and Elaine, who was a stunning black woman with curly chin-length dark hair, was wearing a white and navy striped t-shirt and jeans. The couple came with fresh cloths to replace the pillow that I was holding to Ryan's head. Ryan had grown quite pale, so I hoped the ambulance would get there soon.

"Maura, what happened?", fretted Wilford, as Elaine went into the house to check everything out. "I'm so sorry you got locked in the house, and two of your colleagues are dead? How ghastly!"

I told him the whole tale, leaving nothing out except for the kiss Ryan and I had shared in the library, as he didn't need to know about that.

"Oh, my goodness," said Wilford as I relayed the tale. "I feel awful, because I let Mr. Landry in to write on the wall. I thought he was proposing. If I had told him he had to propose another way, some of this may have been avoided as you all wouldn't have been so terrified from what was written on the wall."

"No, Wilford," I said, reaching out to pat him on the shoulder as he looked shaken. "It's okay. Travis didn't mean to write the horrible words. He was going to just put a congratulatory sign on the wall. Raymond's spirit took him over the second he walked into the house, so that part would have happened no matter what. Please don't feel bad."

I stopped for a second and wondered if I should tell Wilford what Dorothy had told me about my being related to her. He might not believe me, but I felt like I had to tell him and forged ahead with that part of the tale. When I was done, Wilford looked as shocked as I had felt when I first heard.

"If what you're saying can be proven," said Wilford, "that means that you're part owner of Adamson Manor along with Elizabeth's children and grandchildren since you're descended from Dorothy's child."

I gasped. "Wait. Elizabeth's family still lives? I had no idea." My heart leapt with the thought of being able to meet previously unknown relatives.

"Hmm, Dorothy mentioned that she learned about William's adoption to my great-grandparents via a paper that she found in her mother's sitting room," I said. "I wonder if there's any chance it's still there all these years later."

"William," said Ryan. "That reminds me. I almost forgot, what with the head wound and all. His name is on this paper that I brought outside. Maybe it will be helpful."

I grabbed the piece of paper, which I'd forgotten that Ryan had in his hand, from him and took a look through it.

"Oh my gosh!", I exclaimed, giving the paper to Wilford. "Wilford! This is the paper Dorothy mentioned. It says that William was adopted by Harold and Maude Lafferty and those were the names of my great-grandparents. Those exact names can't be a coincidence, can it? They're not that common."

"My dear girl," said Wilford, looking bewildered as he read down the document . "We will of course verify this but considering what happened here today and your connection and conversation with Dorothy, I think I can safely say that yes, you are indeed a true descendant of the Adamsons."

I burst into tears, just as the ambulance came roaring down the driveway and stopped in front of us. What a day! I had found family, but had suffered so much loss in the process.

The EMTs went to work taking care of Ryan, looking at his pupils, asked him some questions, and asked if he had lost consciousness at all. When I replied that he had for a few minutes after he was first struck, they got him settled onto the stretcher and loaded him into the ambulance.

I wanted to ride along with him, but knew it would be better to leave the EMTs to their job, and I could meet them at the hospital in my car after Wilford and I met with the police officers, a man and a woman, who had also just arrived since after all, two people were dead.

Before they left, I went over to Ryan. "I'll meet you at the hospital. Don't worry. You'll be okay and you're in great hands!"

I kissed him lightly on the forehead, and he replied, "Dorothy, I love you. Wait for me. Please don't marry Raymond."

CHAPTER 31

"Dorothy? Raymond?", I thought. "Oh, no. Could it be that he's still affected by Walter's spirit, and that really is the only reason we kissed? Travis did say he feared the possession would continue outside the house."

"Stop it, Maura," I continued, scolding myself. "You're being an idiot. The man was bleeding from the head and is probably delirious. Making sure Ryan is okay is far more important than figuring out if you guys kissed because you wanted to or were motivated by two lovelorn spirits."

After the ambulance took off towards the hospital, Wilford and I entered the house with the two police officers, Officer Jeremy Marcus and Officer Melissa Ross.

"Is there any chance we can prop the front door open?", I asked before stepping foot back in the house. "After being stuck in this house all day and everything that happened, I'm just really nervous about the door not opening again."

I figured that was a better explanation to the police than telling them that ghosts had locked the doors. If I said that, I had a feeling I'd be shipped off to the hospital as well, but to one that requires jackets with sleeves that wrap around the back.

Thankfully, Wilford found two large rocks in the front garden and used those to hold open the double doors. Once those were secured, I felt a bit better about going back inside the house, although I was dreading seeing Kitty and Travis' bodies again.

Wilford directed us into the lower sitting room so I could talk to the police officers. I went to stop him, but then saw that the picture of the Adamson family (my descendants! How crazy) was back up on the wall covering the brutal words Raymond had made Travis write there.

As she was leaving the room, Elaine caught my eye and winked out of view of the police. "Ahh," I thought. "Thank heavens she came in to check everything out and put the frame back up. How on earth did she get the frame back together?"

Wilford and I took a seat on the chaise I had occupied with Ryan earlier that day, while Officers Ross and Marcus sat on the other chaise across from us. I took a glance at the painting and was quite relieved to see that Emma no longer had a scowl on her face.

"So, why don't you tell us exactly what happened here today?", said Officer Ross.

"Where do I even start without sounding like a loon?", I thought. But I remembered Dorothy's wisdom to be brave and I realized what I should say.

"The front door got jammed after we arrived," I started, "and we weren't able to get them open. We tried the other doors in the house, but those all must haven't been used in a while so they had warped and weren't able to be opened from the inside."

"That's correct," concurred Wilford. "I should have warned Miss Hartwell that we only used the front doors, as the others have warped over time and just aren't usable. We really should have replaced them by now, but it hasn't been a priority. I just feel awful about it. As for the front door, that one does get warped occasionally, but a good solid thump tends to open it up."

"It's alright, Mr. Huntley," I replied, grateful that he was backing me up, and continued telling my tale to the officers. "We split up, figuring that we'd have a better chance of getting out sooner if we covered more, and Kitty went upstairs with Travis while Ryan and I checked out the library."

As I played out the scenario in my head, I got teary-eyed thinking of my farewell to Kitty. "We heard a loud noise and ran upstairs thinking that they had found a way out, but sadly, that wasn't the case. Travis and Kitty were trying to move an armoire that was blocking the balcony when Kitty tripped and fell into the mirror, which caused a jagged piece to cut her throat, killing her instantly. She was my best friend!"

I stopped for a second to catch my breath, because I felt on the brink of sobs. Also, I needed a moment to figure out what the heck to say about Ryan's injury as if they asked him separately (which I was sure they would), it wouldn't match up if I made up a story. Ugh!

"After we realized Kitty was dead and we couldn't get out via the balcony," I continued carefully, "we were all distraught and tensions were running high, plus I was feeling claustrophobic. I can't speak for Ryan nor Travis, but they could have been as well. We wound up in the upstairs sitting room, and Ryan and I were upset that Travis tried to move the armoire with Kitty instead of waiting for Ryan. They got into a shoving match due to how upset we all were and Travis pushed Ryan, who fell and hit his head on the poker on the way down."

I could only hope that that would at least somewhat match up with the story Ryan would tell.

"After that, we knew that we needed to get out of the house to get help for Ryan as he was unconscious," I said. "I stayed upstairs with him to hold the pillow against his head to try and quell the bleeding, while Travis ran downstairs to try and find another way out. As I was upstairs, I heard another loud noise. This time, I was warier about thinking Travis had found a way out and didn't instantly jump to that conclusion. I left Ryan upstairs and came down to find Travis underneath the chandelier, which had fallen again just as it did back in the 1940s. I was distraught, went back upstairs, managed to get Ryan carefully down the stairs and tried the door again. Thankfully, this time it did open, which is when I ran to my car and called 9-1-1 and Wilford as our cell phones weren't working in the house." I stopped. "I'm sorry. When I'm upset, I tend to ramble, and this has been quite the upsetting day."

"My poor girl," said Wilford, patting me on the hand. "We all understand, of course. I want to add that as unfortunate as it was that the chandelier fell killing Mr. Landry, I believe that jolt was what caused the front doors to open. I arrived very shortly after Ms. Hartwell called as I live right nearby."

As Wilford spoke, I started to wonder if the doors hadn't been stuck due to ghostly influence wanting to keep us in the house and were instead just stuck due to being old. Oh, my mind was playing tricks on me!

"Thank you for all of this information," said Officer Marcus as he and Officer Ross got to their feet. "We're very sorry for your losses today, Miss Hartwell. To avoid additional pain, we'll go upstairs to see the room that Miss Malloy died in, and then head to the ballroom. Mr. Huntley, if you could fetch your wife to sit here with Miss Hartwell and then show us upstairs, that would be greatly appreciated."

I was so relieved that I wouldn't have to re-see Kitty and Travis' bodies. "Thank you so much, officers," I said. "I definitely feel the need to sit for a moment as everything from the day has hit me by re-telling the events. It's all been a bit too much."

"Mr. Huntley," called Officer Ross to Wilford as he was about to leave the room, "please have your wife bring a glass of water for Miss Hartwell. Thank you."

Turning to me, she said, "I hope that your friend, Mr. Alder, is okay. If it helps, he's being treated at one of the very best hospitals and from what the EMTs said, it sounds like he will be fine. He's very lucky."

Elaine and Wilford came back into the sitting room, and Elaine set a glass of water on the table next to me before sitting down. Once she was seated, Wilford escorted Officers Marcus and Ross out of the room towards the staircase.

"Thank you for the water, Mrs. Huntley," I said. "This has been such a dreadful day. I must ask -- and I'm going to possibly sound crazy -- but how did you get the frame back together so quickly? The last time I saw it, it was shattered in pieces on the floor."

"Please, my dear girl," said Elaine, "you can call me Elaine, especially since it sounds like we're going to be seeing more of each other now that you're a member of our family."

CHAPTER 32

I gasped. "Wait a minute. Our family? You mean you're a member of the Adamson family as well? I had no idea! I thought Wilford was a hired caretaker. And wow, how elitist does that sound?"

Elaine chuckled. "It's okay. That's a common misunderstanding and we actually like it that way because we like to live simply and that's easier to do when people don't know we're rich. Wilford is descended from Elizabeth, as she was his mother. She passed away a number of years ago. The rest of the family doesn't live in town, but Wilford loves this house and couldn't bear to have someone else take care of it, so we have stayed on. Wilford also has a sister, Joanna, and a brother, Thomas."

My mouth dropped open in shock. "I can't believe this. Who else in the family is still alive? Do you and Wilford have children? I want to meet everyone! This is amazing."

"Joanna and her family are all alive," said Elaine. "She married a man named Zachary Ramirez and they had a daughter, Diana. She is happily married to Jerome Cohen and they have an adorable toddler named Jeremy. They all live out in Connecticut with her family, but we see them often."

She continued on, "Wilford and I never had children. It just didn't happen, but we're content with our black labs and seeing the other children. As for Thomas, who lives in California, he and his ex-wife, Amanda, had two daughters, Tanya and Michelle. Tanya and her husband Richard Gable live out in Western Mass, while Michelle and her wife Katherine Talbot, live in California. Everyone comes back here for Christmas, and we try to get together a few other times during the year. You'll be invited to those family get-togethers of course now that you're family."

I burst into tears from happiness, causing Elaine to wrap her arms around me and pull me to her for a hug. For so long, I had no family at all and now I had more than I could begin to comprehend.

"Oh, blessed girl," cooed Elaine, "you must be so overwhelmed. I'm sorry for throwing all of that at you, but I couldn't help myself. I was just going to burst if I didn't tell you. Wilford always says I'm awful at keeping a secret and well, this just proved it."

I sat up straighter and wiped my eyes. Even though the police officers would understand a crying jag hitting me after what had happened today, I still didn't want to come across as a crying mess in front of them.

"I'm so happy," I told Elaine. "I honestly can't believe it. This is all a lot of information to take in, so let's talk about something else for a moment if you don't mind." Elaine nodded, so I continued. "So, the picture frame? What happened there? Was it completely fine and I just hallucinated with everyone else that it fell to the ground and shattered?"

"That was indeed a mess," Elaine said. She stood up and walked over to the closet door in the sitting room. "You weren't having a group hallucination. Thankfully, we wanted to replace that frame anyway, and I had the new one sitting in the closet to change out next week. Well, that timeline got shortened a bit, didn't it? But it worked out well for us, as I know I wouldn't want to have to explain those words on the wall, would you, nor how this happened?" She pulled out a piece of the broken frame, grinned, and tossed it back softly into the closet, shutting the door and firmly locking it behind her, coming back to sit down beside me.

"Oh, those words," I sighed. "Travis meant to put up a cute sign on the wall to congratulate me, but instead he was possessed by Raymond's spirit and Raymond caused him to write that instead."

"Ahh," said Elaine. "That explains it. How dreadful. I hope Raymond's spirit is long gone now, so we don't need to worry about occurrences like that any further?"

"He certainly is," I asserted. "I saw his spirit burst into flames right in front of me, and that certainly looked final."

I wanted to ask Elaine if she, Wilford, or anyone else had ever been impacted by one of the spirits, but as I was about to ask, we heard footsteps coming through the entryway from the ballroom. We were so engrossed in our conversation that we hadn't even heard them come back down the stairs before they went into the ballroom to see that scene. I briefly wondered if they had heard any of our conversation, but nothing seemed amiss.

As Wilford and the police officers came into the sitting room, Officer Marcus spoke. "Thank you for your patience, Miss Hartwell and Mrs. Huntley. We've checked out the house and it appears that your story does indeed hold up based on what we've seen."

Officer Ross added, "We will of course speak with Mr. Alder at the hospital to get his story, but from what we have learned, we shouldn't have any further questions. After that conversation with Mr. Alder, we'll notify Miss Malloy and Mr. Landry's families."

"Thank you," I said, "but it's actually just Travis's family that you need to notify. Oh, please make sure they know that he died trying to find a way out of the house to save us. As for Kitty, she and I bonded because she also lost her parents early in life and was an only child, so there isn't anyone to notify there." I sniffed and turned my head to hide my teary eyes at the thought, feeling ridiculous for doing so, since of course they'd understand and had most likely seen plenty of tears in their jobs.

"Again, we are so sorry for your losses," said Officer Ross. "We will be sending someone from the Coroner's Office over later today. Mr. and Mrs. Huntley, can you make sure that Miss Hartwell gets home or to the hospital to check on Mr. Alder safely?"

"Oh, yes, dear," said Elaine. "We can guarantee she'll always be home and safe with us."

The way she said that caused Wilford to glance at Elaine questioningly as he walked Officers Marcus and Ross out.

"You ARE home right now," said Elaine to me, smiling after they were out of earshot. "So, I wasn't wrong. You're safely here."

Wilford came back in, looked at Elaine, and laughed, saying, "My love, you just really cannot keep any news to yourself, can you? So, I'm assuming, Maura, that now you know that we are related. I hope you know that I couldn't be more pleased! I'm shocked, but I'm very pleased. Welcome to the family!"

CHAPTER 33

I stood up and ran over to Wilford, who embraced me in a bear hug. Elaine came running over as well to wrap her arms around us both with joy.

When we parted from the hug, Wilford turned to me and said, "In case you're wondering, no, none of our doors have ever had issues before today. I made that up entirely on the spot."

Elaine's eyes beamed with pride. "Oh, Wilford, you rascally devil! You are so smart."

"Thank you, Wilford," I said. "I'm glad you told me because I was beginning to wonder if we actually could have gotten out of the house just by thumping hard on the door. I would have been horrified if that were the case, and this all could have been avoided."

"I'm sorry you were worried even for a moment about that," said Wilford.

"No, no," I replied quickly. "It's okay. You were so convincing to the police that you even had me wondering. That's all I meant. I know that two of my friends died today, and I'm saddened by that, but I'm also joyful that I now have lovely family members like you, who I wouldn't have known about had today not happened. So for only that part, I'm grateful."

My head was still spinning from the events of the day, but something was nagging at me and I couldn't figure out what until it hit me. "Oh, my god!", I exclaimed. "The Winter Dance is supposed to happen here tonight, and the catering staff and Ryan's team are set to arrive in an hour to get things moving along. I have to call them all and reschedule the whole thing. We can't have the event here tonight. We just can't."

"It's already handled," Elaine said. "Don't you worry."

"What?", I said. "How? I mean I'm grateful, but how is it all taken care of?"

"As soon as we got your call," Elaine said, "Wilford and I knew we'd have to find another spot for the Winter Dance because it certainly couldn't be held here. Luckily, I'm good friends with the Secretary of the Concord Scout House. So I called her cell and found out the space is luckily available today for putting things together, and also tonight, so I booked it.

"After I fixed the picture here," Elaine continued, "I found the contact info for the catering team and Ryan's guys and gave them all a call, telling them about the change. They all said to please pass along their sympathies. I stopped Ryan's team from going to the hospital to check on him only by promising that he was in good hands and that they could help him out best by making this event go off without a hitch."

"I can't believe it," I said. "You're amazing. Well, I can believe that, of course, but thank you! Thank you so much. What about the guests though?"

"I'm assuming you have a spreadsheet with the guest list and contact info available through your phone," said Elaine. "Email that to me and I'll have the Concord Scout House send out an email to all alerting them to the change, and they'll also follow up with a call."

I pulled out my phone and dashed the information off to Elaine, feeling exceptionally grateful for technology.

"Just to be on the safe side," said Wilford, "I'll put a note up here on the door directing guests to the new location. Elaine also got her friend to ensure the event runs smoothly, so you can go home and rest."

"Oh, no," I said. "I should be there since I've been in charge of this from the start. I don't want to give Ashley any reason to be mad at me." As I said that, I suddenly felt exhaustion take me over. "Any chance you have a Coke here? If you don't, I can just swing by Starbucks on the way over. All I need is some caffeine and I'll rally."

"You most certainly will do no such thing," said Elaine, reaching out to lay her hand on my right shoulder. "I also went ahead and called Ashley. Of course, she was horrified hearing about everything that happened and burst into tears when I told her that Kitty and Travis had both died, poor thing. She's so concerned about you and Ryan. I did tell her that Ryan is being checked out at the hospital, but that he'll be fine. She asked that you go home and get some rest after all you've been through today and she was grateful that the Concord Scout House was able to step in."

"Now," continued Elaine, "let's listen to your boss and get you home to rest. Although first, you should go to the hospital so you can check on your young man."

"Oh," I said, "I'm not sure at all that I can really refer to him as mine. We're not dating and only kissed for the first time today, when I think we were possessed by Dorothy and Walter's spirits. Plus, he called me Dorothy as he was being taken away to the hospital."

"Well," said Elaine, "the only thing to do is to find out. Go see him, look in his eyes, pay attention to your heart, and see what it says. You'll uncover the truth there."

"Thank you," I said, going over and giving Elaine a hug. "I hope you're right."

I went and hugged Wilford as well. "I promise that I'll give you both a call when I get home from the hospital. I'll be fine driving by myself. Being alone for a few moments with the windows down and the music turned up loud after today will actually do me some good."

"Text us when you get to the hospital," said Elaine. "I'm sorry. I'm sorry. I'm sounding like a mother, but I'm going to worry until we hear from you."

"You are so sweet," I replied, "and I appreciate the concern more than you know. It's been a long while since a relative was worried about me, so it touches my heart. I will text you, I promise. Thank you. Seriously."

I walked outside and got into my car. As I did, I glanced up at the Adamson Mansion, still stunned by everything that had occurred today. Despite all the horror and death there, the house (funny that I was now thinking about it as a house rather than a mansion) looked so beautiful and I no longer felt the chill I had that morning. Instead, I felt calm.

But I wondered if that calm feeling would stay when I saw Ryan at the hospital. Had everything that had happened been because he was impacted by Walter's spirit? Or did we have a real chance at love?

CHAPTER 34

When I arrived at Emerson Hospital in Concord, I took a moment to brush my hair and reapply lipstick. There was no fixing my pale cheeks, despite furiously pinching them to try to raise some color, as I must have forgotten to put my blush into my makeup bag this morning.

"Ah well," I thought as I stepped out of my car in the parking garage. "Knowing me, I'll be blushing like a fool anyway, so blush on top of that would look clownish."

I texted Wilford as promised to let him and Elaine know that I'd arrived okay. Then I walked from the parking garage over to the main entrance of Emerson Hospital. The lovely woman at the front desk directed me back to the Polo Emergency Center, which is where the ambulance had brought Ryan. She had called ahead so the Emergency Center staff knew I was coming and led me to Ryan's room.

Ryan was being treated in a private room, so there weren't any other occupants. I was quite grateful for that, as I didn't really want to potentially bring up the topic of spirits, and honestly the whole day, around other people.

He was resting with his eyes closed on the bed, which was raised at the top so he wouldn't have to lie down flat. I was relieved to see that he was wearing his regular clothes since the thought of seeing him in a hospital gown would have been a bit jolting and make me feel like there was something worse going on than a cut on his forehead. I also noticed that he was now sporting a large bandage on the left side of his forehead, where he'd been hit.

Not wanting to disturb him if he was sleeping, I walked over and quietly sat down in the chair next to the bed.

"Maura," I heard as I took a seat. "Hey... Thanks for coming."

"Oh, shit, did I wake you up?", I asked. "I'm so sorry if I did, Ryan. I was trying to be quiet but me being me kind of keeps that from happening far too often and I probably bumped the chair against the bed and jolted you, which woke you up. Smart, Maura. Bump into the bed of guy who's recovering from a head injury. Gosh, that reminds me of when I was volunteering as a candy striper in high school and had to push a guy in a wheelchair who was having an x-ray on his foot. I had never pushed a wheelchair before and wound up knocking that specific foot into the wall. Eep. Okay, right. How are you? How's your head? Did the police interview you already?"

Ryan chuckled. "You're rambling again, Maura, although I'm now bummed you didn't show up in your candy striper outfit. You didn't wake me up. I was just resting my eyes since my head feels like it got a poker slammed into it. Gee, can't imagine why. And yes, the police were here and I talked to them."

I felt better hearing Ryan joking about the poker and the outfit, which showed he was feeling okay at least overall.

"What did you tell them?", I asked. "I hope our stories matched up at least somewhat."

"Well," said Ryan. "I had time on the ride over in the ambulance to figure out what I was going to tell them since I was pretty sure they'd swing by. I basically said that the head injury was an accident -- that Travis and I had an argument because we were so stressed, and we pushed each other. During that, I fell and hit my head on the poker on the way down. Is that hopefully close to what you told them?"

"Gosh," I said. "Yes, that's pretty much exactly what I told them, so our stories correlate. What a relief! Hopefully they won't have any further questions. So, really, how's your head?"

"I have some charming stitches underneath this itchy as hell bandage and will be thrilled when they come out," said Ryan. "But other than that, I'll be fine. Could be one heck of a scar, but hey, it might work out for me, since chicks dig scars, right?"

"Chicks plural?", I thought. "Ouch. Yeah, this isn't the time to mention our potential date, I guess. Okay, so he could just be saying that to suss out how I'm feeling, but ugh."

Feeling deflated, I ignored that question and realized there was a lot that Ryan didn't know that I could tell him instead. "Oh, Ryan, you won't believe this," I said. "You know how I'm an Adamson now after we found that out today, of course. But, you didn't know that it turns out I'm actually also related to Wilford! He is also a descendant of the Adamsons through Dorothy's sister, Elizabeth. Isn't that crazy?"

"Wow," said Ryan. "That's pretty wonderful. I'm glad you've found some family and I'm thrilled for you."

"Thanks," I said. "Quite a day, huh? I still can't believe everything that happened from Kitty and Travis both dying to seeing all the spirits and those scenes thanks to the psychic energy. Not to mention me, you, and Spencer being possessed by Dorothy, Walter, and Raymond. Gosh, what a totally nutty time."

I was doing one heck of an awful job being breezy here. Might as well just announce that I'm breezy next. Oy.

"Right. About that," said Ryan, looking more than a bit uncertain. "We definitely do have to talk."

"Ohhh," I thought. "There are the worst words in history right there."

"It's okay, Ryan," I said. "I know what you're going to say. We were affected by Walter and Dorothy's spirits when we kissed in the library and got carried away by their emotions and thought we felt the same. It wasn't real, of course. How could it have been? We don't have feelings for each other. I've got it."

"No, Maura," said Ryan. "That's not what I was going to say. Well, maybe it was. I don't know. This has been one hell of a confusing day since it's not like one is semi-possessed and also conked over the head every day, right? I need to figure out what was real and what wasn't, and need some time. I hope that's okay."

"Of course," I said, rising from my seat and walking towards the door. "Take all the time you need. It makes perfect sense. I mean, really. We saw actual spirits today. How weird is that? And being affected by them sure does make for a bizarre, confusing day. Okay, I should go. You need to rest. Oh, shit, you still have to get home when you're released and your car's not here. I've got to go, but I'll call Wilford and Elaine and have them bring your car by so you'll have it, or they can bring your car to your place and then they can come pick you up and bring you home. Unless there's someone you want them to call instead to pick you up. Anyway, right. Yeah, they can figure it out. Feel better! I'll see you down the road."

"Maura, wait. Shit…", I heard Ryan say as I fled the room, brushing tears from my eyes only once I was safely down the hall. There was no way in hell I was going to let him see me cry and feel bad for me or feel guilted into a date.

I phoned Wilford and Elaine before I re-entered the parking garage, figuring there wouldn't be much of a signal if any there. Thankfully, Wilford was the one to answer and he didn't inquire why I wasn't staying with Ryan and taking him home myself. What a relief! He promised that they'd take care of everything regarding Ryan and his car and wished me a safe trip home, asking me to text them when I got home safe.

Somehow, I managed to keep the tears at bay (probably thanks to avoiding any sappy songs on the radio by throwing in a CD of AC/DC) until I was inside the security of my house. I sent a text to Elaine, saying "I got home fine. Thanks for taking care of Ryan and his car".

Once that was complete, I considered a long soak in the tub, but I wanted some aromatherapy, and knew I really didn't feel like taking a bath. So, I ran a shower, placing a peppermint/eucalyptus tablet on the floor in the stream of the spray to let the room fill with the crisp, pleasing aroma. When the tab had dissolved, I stepped in, and let the tears flow while I yelled and raged at the day and the loss of Kitty, the loss of Travis, plus the loss of whatever could have been with Ryan.

I turned my phone off, turned on the ceiling fan for white noise (a must every night, regardless of the weather), crawled into bed, and pulled the covers over my head, not wanting to think anymore for the day. My rational side knew that I'd need to face reality tomorrow, but as Scarlett O'Hara said, "Tomorrow is another day." Tonight, I just desperately needed to sleep and be an ostrich, ignoring it all.

CHAPTER 35

The next morning, I woke up to bright sunlight streaming in through my bedroom window, even with the white blinds and blackout light gray curtains up. However, the blackout feature of those curtains only work when I pull them closed, which I hadn't done last night. Oops. Glancing over at the clock, I saw that it was 9:30. I jumped up out of bed.

"Oh, shit!", I yelled. "I'm late for work. Ashley's going to kill me..."

As I spoke, memories of the previous day came rushing back like a slap. I gasped, collapsing back onto the bed.

"Kitty! Travis!", I said. "Oh, my friends. How could I have forgotten what happened even for a moment ! And Ryan. Oh, freaking hell. Ryan. Ugh. I'm such an idiot thinking that kiss was real. He couldn't possibly really like me for me. I mean, c'mon. He was dating Ashley, who looks like a model, and I'm the furthest freaking thing from a model. He doesn't need time. I could give him all the time in the world and he'll still realize that he wasn't interested in me. It was due to Dorothy and Walter. How the hell am I going to ever face him again?"

Remembering that I'd turned my phone off before going to bed, I grabbed it and switched it on. I rubbed my eyes to get rid of sleepies, wondering what fresh hell I was going to find when the phone came on.

For a moment, I pondered leaving the phone alone and going to take a lengthy shower so I could avoid seeing what was there, but knew I'd just be prolonging the inevitable if I did that. Time to be a big girl.

15 texts and nine voicemails? Oh, ugh. What insanity was waiting for me? Okay, texts first.

It looked like 13 of the texts were from Ashley, which wasn't surprising, as she used talk to text, and had a tendency to talk on, but never had enough space in one text for everything, so she always wound up sending multiple ones.

"Maura, honey, what can I say?", her texts started. "I don't even know where to begin and you know that's a rarity for me! I am so sorry about Kitty and Travis both dying yesterday at the house. You guys were such good friends. How awful! You know I loved them and appreciated them so much. They were both one in a million and it's just a tragedy, truly. This is crazy. And Ryan hit his head during a fight with Travis? I just talked to him and he sounds the worst I've ever heard him, but said his head will be fine. So that's good. God, I guess all those ghost stories we've heard about that place were true. And you? Maura, how are you? Ryan told me that you found out you're part of the Adamson family yesterday? Holy shit. Just to add to the craziness of yesterday, huh? I'm just in shock over here and am so sorry that I'm still in Europe and can't give you a big ol' hug and tell you that it will all be okay, because it will. I promise you that. I mean right now it sucks and I have no idea where I'm going with that because of course it's not okay at all at the moment and how the hell is losing Kitty and Travis ever going to be okay? I sound like an asshole even saying that all will be okay, but I hope you know what I mean. Ugh, I need to shut up. But please know I'm thinking of you, and I'm hopping on a plane now to head home. When I get home, I'm coming over there and giving you that big ol' hug and we are having one hell of a stiff drink or a couple, but you are not to come into work for a week, okay? Consider it a paid vacation -- ugh, not that you're going to be celebrating or living it up on the beach. You know what I mean. You have had an awful shock. Couple of shocks, actually. But yes, take the week. Heck, take two weeks if you need it, and get to know the Adamsons and mourn Kitty and Travis and just process all of this. I'm closing the shop anyway for a week. We don't have any events that need to be put on this week or next, so we're good. We all need this time to adjust and heal. I love you, doll. Okay, okay, they're about to take my phone away, so I've got to go. Be well. See, I'm turning the phone off.."

Running my hands back through my hair, I took in everything that she'd said. Selfishly, I was glad that Ryan sounded awful. And a week or two off work? Gosh, I hadn't actually taken any time off since I started at Ellerbee Events, except a sick day here or there or when the office closed down between Christmas and New Year's. Two weeks? Wow.

That would help, though, as I didn't want to see Ryan anytime soon, and that would make that easier. Heck, it sure would give me time to lick my wounds over that embarrassment. Plus, there would be wakes and funerals for Kitty and Travis, and I did indeed want to spend more time with Wilford and Elaine and hopefully some of the other members of the family, too.

Returning to my phone, I saw a text from Ryan. Speak of the devil.

"Maura, call me. Please. I wish our convo hadn't ended like that."

Oof. So much I could read into that if I was that type of person. Okay, fine, I am totally that type of overthinking person. Those three sentences had me thinking that he was feeling guilty for making me feel bad and wanted to apologize, but that he had time to think about it and he wasn't really interested in me and wanted that to be how the conversation had ended, so we were both clear where we stood.

"Screw that," I thought as I deleted the text without replying to it. "We can have that talk when I'm feeling better about things and that day is not even remotely today."

Going onto the next text, I saw it was from Wilford.

"I tried to call. Hope you're doing okay. Unfortunately, news has broken about both of us being part of the Adamson family."

"Oh, no", I thought as I read that text. "Shit. Ashley probably issued a statement to the press about the whole thing since it happened during prep for an event for her company and she didn't realize that Wilford had kept it quiet that he was an Adamson, and I was planning to do the same. I hadn't told Ryan that part, either, so he wouldn't have known to tell Ashley not to say anything. Oof. That's probably what all of these voice mails are about."

Time to face the music as much as I didn't want to. I went to listen to my voice mails, which were close to what I expected. Seven of them were from local reporters, looking for a quote from me on the events from yesterday and/or how I felt having learned I was a member of the Adamson family. One said I must feel like I'd won the lottery, which I thought was a bit morbid considering it was in the same message asking about the deaths of two of my close friends.

The eighth message was from Wilford. "Maura, I hope you get this. I just had a call from a news reporter inquiring about the news that we're both Adamsons. He mentioned that he heard the news from your boss. I know you didn't have anything to do with this news getting out, as you seemed to also want to keep it private and in the family. So, I wanted to let you know about the onslaught of calls or emails you may receive for interviews. Call us when you're ready."

Clicking on the last message, I heard Ashley's voice. "Shit. Shit. Shit. Maura. I'm so sorry. I just landed and got off the phone with Wilford and he's pissed beyond belief that I mentioned your news about being an Adamson and that he's one as well to the press. I didn't realize no one knew he was because I sure wouldn't have said that if I did. Fuck! I feel like I just unleashed the hordes on you. I'm sorry. I'll call them all and give another statement that you need some privacy during this difficult time after the loss of your friends and they should all just call me."

I took a deep breath. "Okay," I said to myself. "It'll be okay. Well, actually, not if they're calling Ashley, since lord knows what else she's going to say. Hopefully some insane story will break today and the reporters will go barking up another tree, making me no longer the talk of the town. If only it were that easy…"

Knowing that I'd find even more craziness in email, I decided to let that particular sleeping dog lie. What I needed to do was go see Travis' parents to express my condolences, although I should probably call them first to see if they even wanted to see me.

After I located his parents' number in my planner, I dialed their number with shaking hands. "Please go to voicemail," I thought. "I have no idea what to say to them right now."

"Hello," I heard Travis' mother, Amy, say. "If this is the press, we have no statement."

"Mrs. Landry," I said quickly. "Please don't hang up. I'm not the press. It's Maura Hartwell."

"Oh, Maura," said Amy. "You must be getting hounded as well by the reporters. I saw your family announcement on the news. Is congratulations the right word, considering what else happened? Probably not. Oh, I don't even know. How are you holding up with it?"

"Please don't even worry about me," I said. "My news isn't important at all today. I wanted to come by to express my condolences about Travis' passing to you and Mr. Landry. You should know that he died instantly, so he wasn't in pain at all. And he was a true hero. The accident happened while Travis was trying to find a way out of the house to get help for a fellow colleague and friend of his, Ryan Alder, who was badly injured. Travis was truly one of a kind and such a great, caring friend. I loved him so much and will miss him forever. Please know how much he loved you two and cherished having you as parents, since he told me so many times over the years."

I could hear Amy stifle some sobs, but she choked them back and said, "Thank you for saying that, Maura. He cared a lot about you as well. At one point, I hoped that friendship would become more down the road, but…" She continued, "Anyway, we would love to see you, but today we have our family coming over. I hope though that you'll be able to come to the wake next Tuesday night or the funeral on Wednesday."

"Yes, of course," I asserted. "I'll be at both to pay my respects. Please know that my thoughts are with you and your family."

"Thank you, Maura," said Amy. "I have another call coming in now, so I have to go."

Hanging up the phone, I burst into tears thinking about Travis and the loss that his parents were going through. Part of me wondered if I should show my face at the wake/funeral, or if that would turn it into a sideshow with all of the paparazzi that could also show up. Would that make things worse? I really wasn't sure.

My phone rang in my hand and I jumped, fearing it was a reporter again. When I looked at it, though, I saw it was coming from Ryan.

"No, no, no," I said to the phone as I deftly rejected the call, sending it to voicemail. "I just had a bad enough call with Travis' parents that's got me all upset. I don't need hearing from you that there's no chance in hell of an us. Yes, I'm sticking my head in the sand here, but I don't care. Just no."

I waited to see if Ryan left a message and was both relieved and bummed at the same time that he didn't.

"Get a grip, Maura," I told myself. "You're going to have to deal with that eventually, but you have other things to do today."

I knew that I owed Ashley a call, but I really didn't want to hear her apologies about sending the reporters at me and spilling the information about my new family ties. So, instead, I went with something that would hopefully make me feel better and called up Wilford and Elaine.

CHAPTER 36

Elaine picked up the phone halfway through the first ring, like she'd been sitting right by the phone. "Maura!," she said. "So good to hear from you. Did you sleep okay, or was your phone ringing all night from the reporters?"

"Shockingly, I slept fine, "I replied. "I actually turned off my phone before going to sleep to shut out the world for a few. Glad I did, because I woke up to the craziness of reporter voicemails. Were you guys harassed all night? If so, I'm SO sorry. I had no idea Ryan would tell Ashley, who would then spill it when she issued a press release about the event. I feel just awful!"

"No, it's okay," said Elaine. "Really. Ashley called us to apologize and said we should also turn off our phones, but she was issuing a blanket 'no comment' on our behalf and yours about our family ties. It seemed to help as we haven't had a call since last night besides your call right now."

"Oh, what a relief," I sighed. "I hope that does the trick because I really want to be able to leave the house at some time today."

"You most certainly are leaving the house today," said Elaine. "What's that, Wilford? Oh, fine. Hold on, Maura. Wilford wants to be the one to tell you."

"Tell me what?," I wondered. But then Wilford came on the line.

"Maura," said Wilford, "So glad you called. I've been on the phone -- my personal cell phone, not our landline -- all night and this morning.

Thankfully, no one seems to have tracked down my cell number yet and hopefully they won't."

"If you weren't talking to the reporters," I asked, "who were you talking to then?"

"Oh, yes," said Wilford. "I was letting my relatives know about their new relative and they're all just chomping at the bit to meet you and welcome you to the family. Johanna and Zachary are coming up from Connecticut along with Diana, Jerome, and Jeremy today. Tanya and Richard are also coming out from Western Mass. And Thomas, Michelle, and Katherine are flying out from California tomorrow. It will be a true family reunion!"

"Wow," I said. "That's wonderful. I mean I'm nervous to meet everyone -- and it sounds like I'm meeting them all at once, which is even more nerve wracking -- but I really hope they love me. Especially since some of them are traveling quite a way just to meet me. Yikes."

"They will love you," said Wilford. "I'm certain of it. Plus, they've all heard only good things about you as Elaine and I can't stop raving about you."

"Oh, gosh," I replied, making an audible gulp. "No pressure there. But seriously, thank you for accepting me into your family so quickly. I know it's been quite a shock for you and Elaine as well having a new family member thrust upon you."

"We are delighted," replied Wilford. "Truly. This probably isn't going to help your nerves about the next time we see you, although I'm saying it to assure you, but you feel like the daughter/child Elaine and I never had."

I chuckled because otherwise I'd sob. "That might be the most heartfelt thing I've heard in a while," I said. "Thank you, Wilford. I only hope you and Elaine continue to feel that way as you get to know me. I do feel a connection to you both and love that you have already shown a really caring side for me, and I appreciate that so much. I'm looking forward to spending much more time with you both getting to know you more and meeting the rest of the family."

"Wonderful!," said Wilford. "I'll put Elaine back on the phone as she's the one who has been arranging everything. We will talk soon, dear."

"Maura, this is so exciting," said Elaine. "So Wilford told you the whole family is going to be in town. Everyone will be here tomorrow, which is Monday, so we were wondering if you could come over to our place on Tuesday sometime during the day. Say maybe 10 or 11 a.m.? Unless of course you have other plans or one of the wakes/funerals that day?"

"I talked to Travis's parents earlier," I said, "and his wake is scheduled for Tuesday night with his funeral Wednesday morning, so earlier Tuesday works. 10 a.m. is fine."

Grabbing my planner, I started to put all three events into there, not that I was about to forget any of them. As I got to jotting down Travis's wake, the doorbell rang.

"Oh, please don't be Ryan," I thought to myself, wondering if I should answer the door or leave it be. "I don't want to deal with this right now…"

CHAPTER 37

"Maura Hartwell, I know you're there!," shouted Ashley from outside my door. "I see your car in the driveway. You open this up right now or I'm breaking it down and you know I'm not kidding, missy."

"I'm coming," I yelled back, as I walked over to open the door and let Ashley in.

"There you are," Ashley said. "So glad I didn't really have to break down the door because I'd probably break a nail and I just had these done, so that would be a shame. Plus, it would be a waste of this bottle of vodka here."

Ashley sashayed into my living room and set down the vodka bottle on my coffee, tossing her coat and purse onto the couch. Then, she spread her arms out.

"Get over here right now for that huge ass hug I promised you," she said.

I complied, gratefully walking over into Ashley's embrace. Embarrassing myself, I burst into sobs.

"Aww. Cry it out, hon," Ashley said, rubbing my back. "God knows you deserve one hell of a cry after everything you've been through. I still can't believe it. And I am SO sorry that I told the reporters your news. I feel like such a jackass -- I just didn't think after jumping on a call right as I was boarding the plane. Helllooo, brain fart. I thought Wilford was going to murder me from how irate he was when I got his message after the plane finally landed."

Taking a deep breath to quell the tears, I was able to speak and stepped out of Ashley's arms. We both sat down on the couch, pushing aside Ashley's coat and purse.

"It's okay," I said. "I mean, I didn't exactly want the news to get out, but I realize how it did. Plus I didn't tell Ryan that neither I nor Wilford wanted it to become public, so I can't really fault him for that."

"Oof, Ryan," said Ashley. "Yeah, he's also really pissed that I went and told the press. He wouldn't speak to me on the way to his apartment this morning. He finally deigned to speak to me when we were in his apartment before I left to come here."

"Wait," I said, my mind spinning. "How did you wind up giving Ryan a ride from the hospital this morning? I thought Wilford and Elaine were going to do that last night."

"Oh," Ashley replied. "The hospital wanted to keep Ryan overnight for observation due to the head injury. So, when I talked to Wilford, he said he was going to go pick up Ryan. But I told him my place was closer to the hospital than Wilford was, so it just made sense."

"Shit," I thought. "Did they rekindle their relationship after all the insanity? How the hell do I ask that?"

"I'm glad you were able to give him a ride and that he was able to go home," I said carefully, trying to avoid hearing something I desperately didn't want to hear. Changing the subject, I continued, "How was Europe, by the way? And ack, I haven't even asked. Did you hear how last night's event went at all?"

"Last night was great," said Ashley. "Don't worry. Every little detail that you planned in advance was so well done that the Concord Scout House was able to execute it perfectly. And it was the highest amount of donations the Historical Society has ever received. As for Europe, it was superb, if I do say so myself. Went off without a hitch. We generated a ton of press, the Kardashians are beyond thrilled, and you clearly are completely wrecked from the events at the Adamson Mansion because you didn't notice this."

Ashley wriggled her left hand up in front of my face and I saw the large diamond-stuffed band that she now sported on her ring finger.

"Oh, my gosh," I said, wanting to vomit, but putting on some semblance of a happy face. "Congratulations! So I guess the engagement is back on? I'm sure you and Ryan will be very happy together."

"You silly goose," squealed Ashley. "This isn't from Ryan. Please, that's old news. I thought he told me that he told you we broke up and I was seeing someone else. Well, that someone else – Carlos Delgado, by the way -- and I eloped over in Europe after the Kardashian wedding was over. It's funny because you had mentioned Ryan and I eloping over there, which is how the thought occurred to me… with Carlos instead of Ryan, obvs. We're going to have a wedding and big to-do here, of course, since that wedding probably wasn't legal since we didn't have a license, but hey, we sure feel married and that's what counts. Okay, it doesn't count to the courts, but we'll get that fixed. I'm just so happy."

Looking at Ashley, I could tell she was really happy. She had the largest smile I'd ever seen on her face and when she spoke about Carlos, her eyes just lit up.

"Enough about me," said Ashley. "Huh, who knew I'd ever say that? Well, there's more, but I'll tell you that later. Now, seriously, how are you? You've had one freaking whirlwind of a few days."

"I really don't know," I replied. "I'm happy beyond belief to get to know Wilford, Elaine and the other members of the Adamson clan. But losing Kitty and Travis… Ugh, I just feel lost without them, and it was just absolutely brutal seeing both of them after they died, and Travis right as he died."

"Ryan told me a bit about that," said Ashley, looking sad. "I know how close you and Kitty were, and you and Travis were good friends, too, despite his interest in making it more. Yes, I knew that. I have eyes. I can't even imagine seeing either of them dead, let alone as Travis died." She shuddered at the thought, and reached over to give me another big hug.

"You will get through this," Ashley said. "I know that sounds trite as fuck, but it's true. It will take a ton of time, of course, and you're never going to forget either of them, but the pain will lessen over time. I've never told you this -- hell, I've never told anyone this -- but a boy I dated in high school killed himself in front of me by shooting himself in the head."

I gasped with horror. "Ashley! I'm so sorry. I had no idea."

"It was a long time ago," said Ashley, "but I can unfortunately still see that scene. We were taking a break from our relationship, and he was upset about it. I found out later from his parents that he suffered from clinical depression, which I didn't know. He called me and asked me to stop by one afternoon after school when his parents weren't home. I thought he just wanted to talk about maybe getting back together, so I agreed. When I got there, the front door was unlocked, which was common, but I called his name. He was upstairs and told me to come on up. As I walked up the stairs to his room, I heard him say 'Ashley, I'll always love you', and then I heard the shotgun go off. He had put the gun in his mouth and blew out the back of his head. It was awful. I was in therapy for years after that to deal with his suicide. So when I say I get what you're going through, I unfortunately really do."

This time, it was my turn to give a big, comforting hug. "Oh, Ashley," I said. "That is just horrific, and that he waited 'til you got there to do so somehow makes it even worse."

"Yes," said Ashley. "For the longest time, I beat myself up wondering what I could have done to stop him, but my therapist finally made me realize that John was fighting his own battles and there was no way I could have known because he never told me. Plus, since he shot himself as I was walking up the stairs, I couldn't have physically tried to stop him. Once I realized that, I was so angry and couldn't believe he'd done that to me. But it wasn't about me. In John's head, it was all about his pain and I was just the person he chose to call. I also had to realize that there was nothing I could have done to save him -- I may have been able to prevent it for a little while had I known, but I couldn't change John. He's the only one that could basically save himself."

"I'm still so sorry you had to go through that," I said, "but thank you for sharing it to let me know I'm not alone in this."

"You are never alone," said Ashley. "I know you haven't had a birth family since your parents passed, but I've always felt like our company was one big family and sadly, now we're mourning the loss of two of our close family members. However, you now have an even larger family of the Adamson clan and I couldn't be happier for you about that. So, tell me, now that you're rich, are you going to still keep working or am I going to lose you?"

"Of course you're not going to lose me!," I replied. "I always told myself that if I ever won the lottery, I'd continue working and that's not going to change from this news. Plus, I really do love what I do at Ellerbee Events and helping make events and dreams/plans come to life."

"I'm so glad to hear that," said Ashley, "because that's the other thing I had to talk to you about -- after groveling my ass off and making sure you were okay."

"What is it?", I said. "Shit. I'm not fired, am I? Wait, that can't be it since you just asked if I'm going to keep working..."

"No, no, no," Ashley quickly replied. "Not in the slightest! I have some news. Carlos and I are moving to Rome and I want you to make Ellerbee Events your own."

"Wait", I yelped. "You're doing what? Like you're moving today? Ashley, I'm not ready for that! Did you see what just happened with the first event I was supposed to produce all on my own?"

Ashley laughed. "No, not today, but you'd be fine if we actually were moving today, you silly goose! We're going to be bi-continental going back and forth between the US and Europe for a year, so I'll still be here quite a bit while also starting to establish my business there. At the same time, I'll be mentoring you to take over and I know that you'll do great. I seriously have no doubt. In a year's time, I'll move to Europe for good and the business will be yours. If you want it, of course."

"Yes!", I shrieked with joy. "I do want it. That's been my dream, but I always pictured it as years if not decades off. Oh, my gosh. I'm thrilled and so glad you'll still be here for a year so I can learn from you."

I jumped up off the couch and ran into the kitchen. "Okay, screw this vodka, as sweet as it was for you to bring it," I said. "I'll put that vodka away for another time. Don't worry. I'll drink it at some point. I have a bottle of champagne tucked away for a special occasion and there is nothing more special than this moment."

"Yummy," said Ashley. "I do love me some champagne, so you know I'm all for that. And you are still taking the next two weeks off, by the way. But after that, it's time to get down to learning everything about running a business. Are you ready?"

"Yes, ma'am," I grinned, bringing back two wine glasses, since I didn't have any champagne flutes, filled with champagne and handing one to Ashley. "I can't believe this is happening."

"You deserve it," said Ashley, "and I know you'll succeed and make this events company a thing of beauty. I was going to say you'll make it better, but it's tough to improve on perfection." She said that last bit with a wink.

Ashley clinked her glass to mine, saying "To new beginnings!", and that felt so right. New family and a new business venture. What else would be new? I tried not to think about Ryan, but it was tough not to wonder if and wish he'd be part of this new life.

CHAPTER 38

The next two weeks passed quicker than I could have imagined. I attended Travis's wake and funeral, and no, they didn't play "Staying Alive". I didn't think it would be right to ask that of his parents. Instead, I blared it in his honor on the way to and from both occasions.

Then, there was planning and attending Kitty's wake and funeral, which had a packed crowd with all of her friends from and fans of her burlesque show. Kitty's wake did have unusual music, including "Lady Marmalade" from the "Moulin Rouge!" soundtrack to honor her burlesque heritage.

She had always promised me that I'd play that at her wake if she passed away before I did, so I couldn't refuse her request when it came time to make the plans. I wondered how it would go over, but it actually turned out to be a good thing as it caused a number of people to start singing along, which prompted smiles all over the place.

Her funeral was more of a somber affair than the wake, but it also had its own Kitty twist. In her memory, I read the poem, "She Is Gone" by David Harkin, which reminded people of how wonderful Kitty was and how fabulous it was that they had known her even if it was for a short time. I loved the meaning behind it, and somehow got through reading it without getting choked up, surprising myself.

When I wasn't attending or planning the wakes and funerals, I spent almost every other waking hour with Wilford and Elaine learning more and more about the Adamsons and also getting to know the family.

Wilford found out something very interesting when he looked into the news about my being a descendant of the Adamson family. He hired a private investigator, with my blessing, to figure out why I'd never known about the Adamsons. In the process, he found out that Richard Wingham had passed on 15 years ago. However, Wingham's son, Martin, had been instructed by his father to do something for him after his passing -- which was to reach out to my mother with the information that she had descended from the Adamson family.

As it turned out, Martin Wingham had met with my mother a few days before my college graduation, and had given her the information that Richard felt comfortable releasing only after his death, as he didn't want to die without the truth of William's adoption coming out. Richard had sent the information to Emma a year after the adoption, but wasn't sure if she ever received it since he never received a reply. As we now knew, that document had been tucked away in Edward's study until Travis uncovered it thanks to Raymond causing him to look for the gun.

When Martin didn't hear from my mother again, he figured she didn't want to be involved with the Adamson clan, so he didn't pursue it. Instead, shortly after that was when my parents died in the car accident. At least now I knew what the news was that my mother was planning on telling me at my graduation dinner. It was nice to have that question no longer unanswered, although I still would have given anything to have my parents back rather than a question answered.

As for the family reunion, the visit from the other Adamson family members went so well. I was quite nervous about meeting them, since I felt like I was intruding on their family and wondered if they'd like me, thanks to my usual lack of confidence making an appearance.

However, I quite surprisingly felt like I was embraced as part of the family from the moment I met them all. I think it helped that my legitimacy as a relation had been finalized by then. If that was still in question, perhaps they would have been a bit more guarded, and understandably so.

But with it settled that I was indeed a relative, I was accepted with open arms. They all wanted to hear everything I could remember about my grandfather, William, and also about my parents and me, too. In return, I asked so many questions about their lives. For once, I just couldn't shut up because there was so much I wanted to know and talking about my parents made me so happy.

It felt like I was home being around everyone in the Adamson family, which was something I hadn't felt in a while, besides when I was around Kitty, of course, who had been like family to me. And they all accepted me for me, which was just thrilling.

When everyone had to leave to head back to their homes, it wasn't as difficult as I thought to say "goodbye" because I knew I'd see them all again soon. Especially since I already had plans lined up and dates set to visit or be visited by all of them. Having a family was truly a dream come true.

Speaking of dreams, I tried my best to not think about Ryan, but my subconscious apparently thought otherwise as he appeared in my dreams most nights. He had called twice, but hadn't left a message and I wasn't about to call without knowing what he was going to say. I knew I was being a petulant toddler about it, but I just didn't want to give up that possibility yet.

It did help that I had Wilford and Elaine to hang out with to learn everything I could about them and the Adamsons. Wilford told me that they were thinking of retiring, and that I could take over managing the mansion if I wanted to. That was a tempting thought because I could then plan and hold events there after Ashley moved to Europe -- and hope they'd go far better than my first one there, which they should considering the ghosts were gone.

I still couldn't believe that I'd found a family. That they were rich was just a further blessing. Yes, I was now quite a bit wealthier than I had ever been previously, but as I'd told Ashley, I still wanted to work and couldn't see myself doing anything but that. The money could be saved for my retirement years, when I wanted to just plan events part-time or here and there.

That didn't mean I didn't go shopping a bit more than usual, though. I'm only human. Plus, retail therapy was a great way to try to forget about Ryan. Key word there being "try".

CHAPTER 39

The Sunday before my first day back at work in two weeks came with torrential downpours. That didn't stop me from getting in one more retail therapy binge, though. Post shopping, I got in my car in the Target parking lot, tossing my bags in the trunk and my now soaked umbrella onto the floor of the backseat. As I did so, I glanced at my phone. I never bother to look at my phone/try to make a call while in the store because the cell signal is so bad and changes from aisle to aisle.

For once, it looked like my phone had been busy while I was in the store -- I had a missed phone call from Ryan without a voice message, followed by two texts from him that said simply, "Please call me." and "Maura, it was real for me. It still is."

That last one got me teary-eyed and I wondered if I'd made a mistake. Was it really possible that Ryan did have feelings for me and he wasn't just influenced by Walter's spirit? It had now been more than two weeks after the Adamson Mansion, so that couldn't still be lingering.

"Aargh. I'll think about calling him or not on the way home," I promised myself, putting my phone back in my purse and setting that on the passenger side floor so I wouldn't be tempted to look at his texts again while I was driving. No need to join my friends in the afterlife by getting in a car accident.

I turned on the radio, which was on the oldies station, and sang along to Lenny Welch's "Since I Fell for You" for a few moments, until I realized that tears were running down my cheeks.

"Oh, lovely," I said to myself. "Who looks like a crazy woman driving and crying? Okay, and now people are going to pass by, seeing me driving, crying, and talking to myself. Get a grip."

Changing the channel, I apparently couldn't get rid of the oldies, as "Crying in the Rain" by the Everly Brothers (that irony sure did give me a grin) was on the next station followed by "Forget Him" by Bobby Rydell and "Since I Don't Have You" by The Skyliners. Neither of those were going to quell the tears, so I reached over and switched to see what CD I had in the player. Ahh, yes, a little "Fiddler on the Roof" would do just the trick. Specifically "If I was a Rich Man" and "Matchmaker", which were both perfect to caterwaul along to when I wanted to sing at the top of my lungs.

I'd just have to change back to the radio or another CD before "Anatevka" came on -- that song about a woman leaving her parents and not knowing when she's going to see them again always makes me bawl as it hits a wee bit too close to home. Although I sure did feel like a "stranger in a strange new place", especially without having Kitty to turn to these days.

"Aww, Kitty," I said (yes, still talking to myself in the car, people who are driving by. Ignore it). "I wish you were here. I would love to get your advice on this and if there's even an inkling of a future there with Ryan or if this is all just wishful thinking on my part."

Right then, the CD stopped playing and switched over to the radio, which was now playing "Walkin' on Sunshine" by Katrina and the Waves. I couldn't help but chuckle.

"I knew you were here with me, Kitty," I said. "Thank you. Thank you. Thank you for continuing to be with me and for that sign."

Yes, for all I knew, it was just a mechanical error because I've seen wonkiness happen with my radio changing stations before when I had the "Country Strong" CD in the car, but not when the CD was actually playing. Maybe I just needed a new sound system, but whatever the case, it was just the sign I was looking for, and the timing certainly was everything, as it always is.

I happily sang along to the radio, which thankfully continued to play all upbeat music all the way home. As I turned onto my street, I saw a taxi cab pulling away from my house, and a tall man standing at my door with a bouquet in one hand, and an umbrella in his other that shielded his identity from me, but I knew who it must be.

My heart leaped out of my chest as I pulled quickly into my driveway. Not even waiting to get my bags out of the trunk (thankfully I hadn't purchased any food that could go bad), I sprinted out of the car to my door.

"I'm here!", I yelled over the rain to the man at the door. "Oh, I'm so glad you didn't leave."

He turned, and I lost my breath.

CHAPTER 40

It wasn't Ryan waiting for me at my house. It was Spencer, looking as dashing as usual in a light gray button-down shirt, dark gray tweed vest and dark blue jeans. No! It couldn't be. Hilariously enough, after all the years of agonizing over him, I realized that I had quite frankly forgotten about him with everything that had happened.

"Well, I'm happy to see you, too, darlin'" said Spencer. He leaned over to kiss me hello, and I hope I didn't visibly recoil as I turned my head so his lips would meet my cheek instead of my lips in return.

"Oh, have you got a cold?", continued Spencer. "Yeah, I don't want to catch that if you do. How about we go into your house so we don't get drenched standing here?"

Feeling mute, I simply nodded and unlocked the door, running off to the bathroom to grab us both a towel to dry off.

"Give me a second, Spencer," I said. "I just want to change really quick because my clothes are soaked."

"No problem," Spencer said, hanging his jacket up on the coat rack right inside the front door entrance. "I can just make myself at home... unless of course you want to take a shower together instead to really warm us both up?"

"No thanks. I'm already soaked to the skin and right now I just want to dry off," I replied, walking off to the bedroom and gently closing the door and locking it behind me. No need for him to try the door and find it unlocked so he could walk in while I was changing, thinking I was coming on to him.

I rubbed my hair with the towel, letting it fall into curls from the rain. Then, I stripped off my wet clothes, grabbed my comfiest pair of black leggings and an oversized hunter green sweater and quickly put them on along with black fluffy socks.

"Okay, you can do this," I told myself. "Find out what he wants and get him the hell out of here so you can call Ryan and figure that whole thing out."

Walking into my living room, I found Spencer sitting on my couch like he owned the place. He must have dug around in the kitchen cabinets as he'd found a glass vase that he put the flowers in and set it on the Lane hope chest/coffee table along with the towel, which I grabbed and threw into the hamper in the laundry closet before coming back out to talk to Spencer.

Realizing that I hadn't even glanced at the bouquet, let alone thanked him for them (I guess I didn't care much about my manners), I walked over and picked up the vase. When I noticed they were red roses, I had to stifle a wry chuckle. Yup, that was about right. Spencer finally does what I wanted him to do forever and shows up at the door with flowers out of the blue and they're the ones I hate the most.

"Thanks for the flowers, Spencer," I said, offering a forced smile. "They're lovely. However, I'm not sure what the occasion is, though. It's not my birthday or an anniversary since we don't have an anniversary, so..."

"Can't a guy give a lady flowers without there being a reason?", asked Spencer. "Okay, you know me too well. Of course I have a reason. I was up in Maine at the ski lodge, and happened to see your news on tv a few weeks ago. When I was back, I had to rush right over to congratulate you."

"My news? Congratulate me?" I wondered to myself what he was talking about because I knew I hadn't actually ever gotten a chance to tell him about the event I was producing at the Adamson Mansion, and that's the only thing I could think of that would get well wishes. At the thought of the Adamsons, light dawned.

"Oh, lord, you mean that news story about how I'm related to the Adamsons, don't you?", I said. "I still can't believe that became an actual news story. Must have been one hell of a light news day. Yes, it turns out I'm related to the family through my mother, who's descended from one of the Adamson daughters. Members of their family are still alive, and I have been spending time with them and have been brought into their fold. So I'm part of a family again, which is pretty shocking, but I'm beyond thrilled because they're all great. However, I found out about it in a horrible way with Kitty and Travis' death occurring at the same time."

"You have no idea what this means for us, do you?", said Spencer. "Honey, you're freaking loaded! That makes you a catch! I had to come over as soon as I got back to make sure no one else scooped you up. Just think -- we can sell that old mansion off and move to Bora Bora, or we can go live in the place, after we restore it, of course, and have butlers and maids waiting on us hand and foot. It will be perfect."

I was pretty stunned into silence by what I was hearing. Taking it as a sign of interest, Spencer came over to me, took my hands, and looked intently in my eyes.

"That's what you've always wanted, right, Maura?", said Spencer. "You can stay home and I'll manage your wealth or hell, I'll hire someone to do it. We'll be together and freaking rich, doll! And neither of us will have to work ever again."

As he said that, I could see a cozy scene play out in my head of a happy couple living in the Adamson house and sitting and having coffee in the library. It really did sound simply lovely and appealing, minus the whole not working at all thing. However, there was just one teeny little problem. It wasn't Spencer in that picture in my head -- it was Ryan.

I took my hands out of Spencer's and said, "You know. I thought that's what I did want for years. Well, more specifically, I thought that it was YOU I wanted, but it's not at all. I don't want to move to Bora Bora. If you knew me at all, you'd know that I actually love to work and plan on continuing to work, and I'm certainly not going to tear down nor do anything to restore the Adamson Mansion as it's beautiful as it is, despite what happened there. Lastly, I don't want you anywhere near let alone managing any money I have, because I don't trust you as far as I can throw you. Honestly, Spencer, I hate to say this, but I pretty much forgot you existed these past two weeks until you showed up at my door."

Spencer sputtered and looked like he was going to say something, but I continued on now that I finally had the confidence to officially say goodbye to him in person instead of being a coward and saying my farewell in email like I had before.

"Spencer, if you had told me this five years ago -- or hell, even just a year ago or a few months ago, sadly enough -- I would have jumped for joy into your arms and happily agreed. But that's not who I am anymore. I told you in that email I sent that I wanted more and I meant it. Of course, you paid no heed to what I wrote because you figured you could just dangle some pretty words at me and you'd get what you want. That's not enough anymore and it never should have been. What we had was never love. How could it have been? It was a crush on my part that went on way too long and involved me turning you in my head into someone who could be what I wanted. Thank heavens I've finally realized that was just a foolish schoolgirl's romantic notion of trying to make a daydream real. It wasn't real. You don't love me. You don't even care about me. You just keep me around because you like knowing I'm there."

"Baby," interrupted Spencer. "How can you say that? Of course I care. I'm here, aren't I? And we're going to live happily ever after and all that fairytale true love shit."

"Are you even listening to yourself?," I replied. "Sure, you're here now, but you're here because you heard I'm rich, and that makes me ill. If you really cared, you would have asked me how I am doing considering that I had a horrifying experience of being trapped in a house where two of my friends, including my best friend in the world, Kitty, actually died. By the way, Kitty is someone who you've met a few times, but I'm sure she was just a person in the background to you because she didn't fawn all over you nor fall for your crap. Why didn't you even think to ask about that? And I certainly didn't see you at either Kitty's wake nor the funeral. Right. Right. You were up in Maine having the time of your life. Why interrupt that for the wake and funeral of the best friend of someone you proclaim to care about? Someone who actually gave a flying fuck about me would have been there for me to support me at Kitty's wake and funeral or at least show up. But you weren't there. Why is that? Oh, that's right. It's because you don't give a shit. All you care about is Spencer and what Spencer wants and that doesn't fly for me anymore. At all."

Spencer went to interrupt again, but I continued on, ignoring him, which was well past time.

"I don't care if this sounds like I'm asking for the world, but I want true love, and no, real true love isn't fairytale shit as you so appallingly just called it. I don't want just lust. Not someone who wants to spend forever with me just because I'm now wealthy, but before that wasn't even worth a swipe right on Tinder because you knew you already had me wrapped around your finger. Dammit, I deserve someone who cares about me and actually talks to me and wants to know what I'm thinking instead of just seeing me as a meal ticket to an early retirement. And you know what, Spencer? I think I've possibly found a guy like that -- but he sure as hell is not you. Even if that man who I love doesn't love me in return, I still wouldn't go back to the old me who followed you around like a puppy, begging for attention and lapping up the slightest offerings. I'd say I'm sorry for telling you all of this, but I'm not because it's well past time that I did. Now I want you out and to leave me alone. Spencer, we're really and truly over. And don't try to now go swiping right on me, because you won't find me on any dating sites. Now I'm asking you nicely. Please leave."

I walked over to the door, taking Spencer's coat off the hook and handing it to him along with his umbrella as I opened the door to escort him out.

"You are making a big mistake, Maura," said Spencer. Ah, there was the Spencer I knew all too well coming out. "This isn't you. I know -- it's gotta be this whole thing. It's messing with your head and made you think you need to turn against me. Baby, you're going to realize that I'm the best you're going to get because no one else is going to want you. One day you're going to wake up, turn around, and wish you'd played today quite different."

"For the longest time I thought that you were everything I wanted," I said thoughtfully. "But, I was wrong and you're wrong. I deserve and will get soo much better than you. Of course, that's not saying much because you just threw little scraps my way, so really anything would be better than that. If heaven forbid I wake up thinking one day that I should have said 'yes' here, I'll quickly remember that I turned down the thought of a very shallow, meaningless life with you in pursuit of something that could be real and I'm okay with that. And the fact that you're standing here trying to tell me that YOU are the best I'm ever going to get pisses me off because it shows just how little you think of me. Now, get the fuck out."

"Well," said Spencer, as he stepped out into the now-dry early evening. "Alrighty then. So, are there any hot, rich, single females in the Adamson clan that you could pass my number to? If so, feel free! You can give a reference of my skills to them."

I laughed as I slammed the door. Ugh, that didn't need a response at all as much as he was probably hoping for one. Let him have the last word. Yeah, clearly Spencer wasn't too distraught by my turning him down if he was sniffing around for other single females he could prey on. Yeesh. I turned away from the door, went into the living room, gathered up the roses, and happily tossed them into the trash.

Still holding the vase, I went to put it back into the cabinet, but the doorbell rang. "Ugh! What the hell does he want now?", I thought as I walked to the door.

As I opened it, I yelled, "What the hell do you want? Did you not get the message loud and clear that I am NOT interested?". Only as the words came out of my mouth did I see that it wasn't Spencer standing there, but Ryan.

CHAPTER 41

"Whoa!," said Ryan, looking horrified and simply amazing in a navy Henley, well-worn blue jeans, and Chucks. "Sorry for disturbing you. Message received loud and clear. I'll leave."

"Oh my god, Ryan," I gasped. "Shit. No. Don't leave. Please don't leave. I thought you were someone else at the door when I said that. Come in. Seriously."

I pulled his arm to drag him into the house before he could walk away from me.

"That's a relief!", Ryan said. "Although not for whoever the intended recipient was of that pretty vivid not interested message."

"That would be my very horrifying ex, Spencer," I said. "He came sniffing around, and I sent him packing."

"That's what I figured," said Ryan. "I actually thought it was Spencer because I passed him leaving in an Uber as I pulled up to your house. Now normally, I'd be embarrassed to admit I know what he looks like, but I'm actually comfortable telling you that I totally googled him after hearing his name from Ashley. And, I've got to say that I'm very glad you sent him packing and are not interested in him anymore since I heard he was a massive douchebag and he kind of looks like one, too."

"Oh, god," I put my hands up to my eyes, cringing while I mentally went through all of the stories Ashley had heard over the years about Spencer and could have told Ryan. "I can only imagine what stories you've heard…"

"It's in the past now," Ryan assured me. "Hell, we both have a past, but they are firmly in the past for a reason. Don't worry about it. Seriously."

"Oh, before I forget," said Ryan, "these are for you, and I see you have a vase here handily enough, but these don't actually require water."

Confused as to what flowers don't need water, I glanced down and started laughing when I realized they were chocolate tulips.

"How perfect!", I exclaimed. "I love them and they're just the most beautiful, delicious-looking flowers in the world. How on earth did you know how much I love tulips, though?"

"Everything you said in the mansion is emblazoned in my memory, Maura," said Ryan. "When we were in the library, you told me all about how you love tulips and hate roses. I was going to get some real tulips, but found these first and thought they were fantastic."

I was stunned. He really had been listening to what I said and stored it away. No guy had ever done that for me before, which didn't say a lot for those guys, now that I thought about it.

"Let me just put this vase away," I said. "I had it out because Spencer had brought over roses, which are now where they belong in the trash, and I was going to store the vase away when the doorbell rang."

Ryan gently took the vase out of my hands and set it on the table. "First, I realized I forgot to say hi. So hi there, you. You look beyond adorable, by the way. I've missed you." He took my face gently in his hands and brought his lips to mine for a light, but tantalizing, kiss."

As our lips parted, I sighed, biting my lower lip. Ryan grinned, saying, "I'll take that as a sign that it was okay to kiss you and you're not going to kick me out. I was wondering."

I remembered the reason for our first kiss in the library and broke away from the embrace, holding Ryan at arm's length.

"I am completely fine with that kiss," I said, "and I have no plans to kick you out. Think I've filled my kick people out quota for the day anyway with Spencer. But we do need to talk. I want to make sure that it's 100% you kissing me instead of Walter kissing Dorothy."

"Why don't we sit down?", said Ryan. We both sat on my couch, and he continued. "When we were in the house, it was so odd because I know I was me and I was in control of my actions, and I remember being attracted to you, like I've also been when I see those moments of you being your true self while the group was hanging out. But I also had this strong feeling of love for you that literally came out of nowhere, which is how we wound up kissing in the library. I just wanted to protect you and treasure you and just kiss the hell out of you, and I had no idea where that came from because it was so out of the blue. Now, I realize that was probably Walter's feelings for Dorothy taking over in that moment there."

My face fell at the last sentence. "I had a feeling that was the case, especially since you called me Dorothy as you were being taken away in the ambulance and told me not to marry Raymond."

"I said what?", said Ryan. "Oh, my god. Well, no wonder you acted the way you did at the hospital. I couldn't figure out what happened there and it makes sense now. Holy shit, Maura, I wish you had told me. I feel awful about that. The only excuse I can give for that is the head conk I had received, which knocked me for quite a loop, and I was just out of it and my subconscious was still messed up from being affected by Walter's spirit."

"It's okay," I said. "I get it. I mean I didn't at the time. I was really hurt then, but I do have to understand that's what happened. And yes, I know we were definitely affected by Walter and Dorothy at the house, which is why I wanted to give you some time without contacting you to help you get rid of any lingering feelings that were there from Walter. If I wasn't around, I wouldn't confuse things further for you."

"I understand that," said Ryan. "I do. But I still wish you'd told me about what I said when I was being loaded into the ambulance. I felt awful when you left the hospital, because you looked so upset and I was gob smacked as to what I could have said to cause that look on your face."

"Well," I admitted, "at the hospital, you also said that you were okay with possibly having a scar -- which, by the looks of it, there won't be a huge one, since that seems to be healing well -- because chicks dig scars. I took that to mean that you were looking for any and all chicks to be interested in you because of the scar. And even as I'm saying that out loud, I'm realizing I'm an idiot and it was a leap."

"You think?," said Ryan. "I'm not saying you're an idiot. Okay, if you are, we're both idiots because I said that about chicks digging scars as you looked freaked, so I thought you were horrified that we kissed, and I didn't want to freak you out more by asking you out again. Now I know that was because I called you Dorothy. But I didn't know that then, and I didn't want to scare you off further by saying that I hoped you specifically like scars. Had to protect my fragile male ego, ya know."

"Oh, lord," I said, laughing at the absurdity of it all. "Okay, so basically if we had just talked then and there, we could have cleared that up weeks ago. So, we're both jackasses. And for the record, I think scars add a touch of masculinity, so yeah, it's a good look on you. But you're already pretty damn masculine already with those arms of yours."

"Ahh," said Ryan. "So, you like my arms, do you? I like hearing that. Well, now I suddenly feel like flexing. And thank god you like arms instead of abs, because I hate to tell you, but I don't have a six-pack nor a 12-pack for that matter. I mean clearly I stay in shape, but my six-pack days are far behind me."

I reached out, placing my left hand on his right upper arm. "Yeah, I am definitely an arm girl and this one is mighty damn fine. You've always looked great to me, so shut it about not having a six-pack."

Before I could add to that, I realized there was still something I still needed to discuss. "So, this all leads to the question I know I don't want to ask, but have to: Is Walter still sticking around you and that's why you're here? I hope you know that Dorothy's not here at all. She left at the house."

"No," said Ryan. "I promise you this has nothing to do with Walter and Dorothy. That kiss may have happened because of them, but I'm here because of you, Maura. Simply you. I have not been able to stop thinking of you since the house, and that's the truth. I still remember seeing you dancing around the house when I first arrived and how just hot and full of life you looked. I was standing outside of the house then, so that wasn't Walter at all. That was me. Yes, things got confused and we were caught up by Walter and Dorothy's spirits in the library, but everything I said I meant."

"So, you're really here as you," I said. "I know I keep asking the same question, but I feel like I need that confirmed because I'm not going to believe it otherwise."

"Yes, Maura," said Ryan. "Walter left me the minute I left the house. I know it because I feel more like me instead of wondering why I'm doing things or why I'm saying something that I didn't expect to, you know?"

"I do get that," I said. "I know we both acted in a way we didn't realize we were going to in the library, and it seemed out of character, but now maybe it wasn't all that surprising. At the time, though, it was, especially since I thought you were engaged to Ashley."

"Oh, I know," said Ryan. "Actually, Ashley was the one who partially prompted me to come here today. I was having brunch two days ago with her and Carlos, who's a great guy by the way, and she's never seemed happier. It's weird because she and I were engaged so it should have been odd seeing her with someone else and talking to her about my feelings for someone else. But I felt comfortable telling her that I couldn't stop thinking about you and thought I'd messed things up badly somehow based on the hospital. I was pretty depressed about it to the point that I was just mindlessly swiping on Tinder the night before and was swiping left on everyone because they weren't you and couldn't compete with the person I wanted, which was you. And then I saw your name and face come up on my screen. I couldn't believe my eyes, and it felt like my heart stopped, because you must not be interested in me if you're on Tinder. However, I took a chance and I swiped right but then didn't get a match, so I figured that I didn't stand a chance with you."

"Wait," I said. "I'm not on Tinder. I haven't been on there in months. Seriously. Hold on."

I went and grabbed my phone out of my purse and pulled up the app. Quickly, I opened the app and sat back down next to Ryan, thinking for a second that I sure hoped Spencer hadn't finally swiped right on me, causing a match to come up from my swipe months back. That would be easy to explain, but I just didn't want to. Thankfully there were no matches. So, I started swiping left on each picture that came up. And then, 30 profiles later, there Ryan's face was looking up at me from my phone.

"Oh, boy," I said, looking at Ryan. "If you're lying and didn't actually swipe right on me, I'm going to be pretty pissed, so speak now…"

"Swipe right," said Ryan. "I promise you I did and you'll know it's true and that you really can trust me in just a moment."

"Aah," I said, swiping right, and then quickly closing my eyes. "I can't look!"

"Open your eyes, Maura," chuckled Ryan.

I opened my right eye, like I was trying to partially hide from a scary scene in a movie, and saw "Instant Match" there on my phone.

"Holy shit," I said. "You really did swipe right on me. Wow."

"Here's what you're going to realize," said Ryan. "I will always tell you the truth and I will happily spend the rest of my life proving that to you. And now I'm going to tell you what Ashley told me when I was basically whining to her about you."

"Should I close my eyes again for this?", I joked.

"Funny girl," Ryan replied. "It's not that scary. Actually, I think you'll like it. So, Ashley stopped me while I was telling my sad tale of not getting a match from you on Tinder. She looked at me and told me to go to see you because when I was talking about you, I had a look in my eyes that she'd never seen the whole time she and I were dating. Apparently, my eyes lit up and I was glowing, in her words, whatever the hell that means. I'm going to assume she doesn't mean I'm now radioactive and that it's a good thing. She went on to say that if there was even a chance that you felt at least half of what she could see I was feeling, then I needed to give it a try."

"That might be the sweetest thing I ever heard," I said. "Although yeah, it's kind of weird coming from your ex, who's also my boss to make it even more bizarre."

"Oh, it gets better," Ryan replied. "She told me that before I went to see you, I needed to think things through and make 110% sure that I was all in for a relationship because despite, and really because of, Spencer's asshattery, you're not the kind of the girl that one just dates and strings along. You're the type that a guy cherishes and even marries. And then she told me that if I didn't try to pursue you or if I did and I hurt you, she was going to maim me and also I'd be unhappy for life not having given us a real try."

"Whoa," I laughed. "Well, first, thanks to Ashley for all of that. And, basically Ashley is going to be pissed if this doesn't work out. Well, I certainly don't want to be the cause of you being maimed."

"Thank you for that," chuckled Ryan, running his hand back through his hair. "So, what do you think? Could we go out on a date and see how that goes?"

"I want to," I said. "Very much, and I do understand that you're no longer being influenced by Walter. However, now I'm just worried that you're at least partially interested in me because I'm wealthier now than I was. That's why Spencer showed up, by the way -- only because he found out the news that I'm part of the Adamson family and he wanted to get rich quick."

"Okay, I'm glad I didn't know that when I saw him," said Ryan, "because I would have stopped the car and slugged that asshole for treating you that way. No, trust me, I'm not interested in you for your money."

"I hope you get that I'm wary because of that," I said. "And then there's the lovely part of me that thinks a guy could only be interested in me because he's possessed by a ghost or only wants me for my money."

"Maura," said Ryan, taking my hands into his. "I want to be the one to help you realize that you are gorgeous, funny, and that any guy in his right mind would be lucky to have you. I'm so sorry that you thought I was only interested in you because of Walter's ghost. As for the money, umm, no, that's definitely not something I need. At all."

"Okay, spill," I said. "That's an order, because it sounds like there's more there."

"Ugh," said Ryan. "I really usually don't tell anyone about this, but I know it's not going to change your interest in me one way or the other because you're already wealthy. Well, the Alston Department Stores -- my great-great grandparents founded them. They named it after my great-great grandfather's last name of Alder and my great-great grandmother's last name of Weston. And those stores grew and grew, and I have a family trust that I came into when I was 21. So, basically, I come from money and could not work if I wanted to quite easily, but I want to keep working as I love working with my hands."

"Oh, wow," I said. "Well, we're alike that way in that I plan on continuing to work as well because I love making events happen and couldn't imagine not working. I'd grow bored really quickly."

"Exactly," sighed Ryan. "I'm so glad you feel the same way, because I've never told anyone about that. Hell, Ashley never even know. She might have guessed but she never said anything. I didn't want women to want me just for my money -- well, that and my dashing good looks."

"Shut it, you," I grinned. "Okay, so we're both rich, so dinner in Paris on a private jet is the usual first date, right? Kidding! I'd actually much rather go walk around some cool museum or go bowling and grab a pizza if that's okay with you."

"That sounds really perfect," said Ryan. "Hell, anywhere where I can spend time being with you and talking to you sounds excellent to me."

"Wow, keep it up, mister," I said. "Those words are definitely working their magic on me."

"Oh, is that so?," said Ryan, inching closer to me. "Hmm, I wonder what a kiss would do then?"

"Let's find out," I said boldly, bringing my face to his.

Ryan's lips met mine, and once again his thumb gently stroked my cheek as we kissed. I was amazed at how hot such a simple move could be.

As we parted for a second to catch our breath, I realized Ryan was humming, and my heart stopped for a moment, thinking he was humming "Smoke Gets in Your Eyes" like he had in the library, although it didn't sound like it. I pulled back.

"What's wrong?," said Ryan. "Are you okay?"

"That song," I said. "What were you just humming?"

"Oh, geez," said Ryan. "Okay, this is embarrassing, and lord, don't laugh, although I don't blame ya if you do. But I was thinking about you all last night and then this morning, and was watching 'When Harry Met Sally' of all things earlier today during my musings. Yes, I'm a sap! Well, the song 'It Had to Be You' has been stuck in my head ever since. That ending scene on New Year's when Harry goes to find Sally to declare his love because he doesn't want to spend one more moment without her is basically what motivated me to hightail it over here to see you. So I guess the song is still an earworm. Had no idea I was humming it."

"Thank heavens," I laughed. "I thought you were humming 'Smoke Gets in Your Eyes' a la Dorothy and Walter again. And that movie gets me every time. I know exactly the scene you mean and I'm kind of loving that it made you actually want to get over here to see me."

Ryan chuckled. "No, no, I promise I am never ever humming that song again. This one's all because of me and you and that's it. I'm here because I want to be here with you, Maura."

"I believe you," I said, pulling him back to me. "Now, get over here and kiss me some more, or we could go grab some food. But to be honest, I really just want to kiss you again first."

"I love hearing you say that," said Ryan, running one hand through my hair and the other down my back to bring me closer to him. "Food is good, but kissing you is even better, and hell, we will have a gazillion dinners in the years to come together."

"That sounds so great," I sighed, falling into our kiss. "Please, let it be so," I thought before I stopped thinking for a little while.

CHAPTER 42

Two Years Later

"Maura," I heard Ashley yell from the door. "The wedding starts in 20 minutes. Is everything ready?"

"They better be, since you're the one running this one for me," I said as I turned towards the door in the master bedroom of the Adamson Mansion, pivoting away from the full-length mirror in my long white tank style A-line wedding gown with a tulle overlay on the skirt. "Now, don't you dare mess up any detail of my wedding day."

"I wouldn't dare," grinned Ashley, who was wearing a navy skirt and jacket (she'd left her signature pink hue behind when she moved to Europe) that clung to her eight months pregnant belly, as she came in and picked up my rhinestone and pearl vintage floral vine bridal hair comb off the vanity table to the side of me. "First, Ryan would kill me and second, I've waited for this day to happen since Ryan got all googly-eyed over you in front of me."

"Aww, I still love hearing that story," I said. "I know I've thanked you a gazillion times for sending him my way, but thank you again and again and again. I've never been happier and I'm so glad you came back from Europe to run the show for me and to be here on my wedding day."

"I wouldn't be anywhere else," said Ashley, giving me a gentle hug. "You deserve this happiness, kid, and it's perfect. I'm so freaking proud of you. Couldn't have left my business in better hands, because you've done so well with it. I'm in awe."

She went to stand behind me, turning me back towards the mirror as she took the comb and inserted it on the right side of my hair above a twisted section that came from both sides and then flowed down in long waves (thank you, extensions!).

"You look so beautiful," said Ashley. "Aww, I'm going to cry!"

"Don't you dare!", I laughed. "If you cry, I'll cry and I don't want to wreck the makeup artist's work."

"Knock, knock," said Elaine as she stood at the door. "Okay if I come in?"

"Gosh, yes," said Ashley. "I have to go make sure the groom is running on schedule and that everything's in order. An event planner's work is never done. I'll see you downstairs, babe." She left the room and closed the door behind her in case somehow Ryan came walking down the hall.

"Oh, thank you for being here, Elaine," I said, as we gently hugged hello so we wouldn't muck up my dress nor her light blue sheath dress with a matching lace overlay. "It means so much to me. Since my parents can't be here, I'm honored that you and Wilford are here, along with my other Adamson relatives."

"Your parents are here watching over you," said Elaine. "I have no doubt whatsoever of that. And I know they're so proud of you and are beaming at how happy and beautiful their little girl is on her wedding day."

I felt tears spring up, so I looked up at the light to try and stop them, unsure if that would actually work although I'd read that somewhere.

"Goodness," said Elaine. "What have I done? Here, let's dab your eyes with this little tissue. It's perfect for fending off those tears without marring your makeup. We don't want you looking like a raccoon walking down the aisle."

That image caused me to laugh, which lightened the mood considerably. "That would be hilarious," I said. "I can only picture the look of confusion on Ryan's face if I did that."

"That's our girl," Elaine said, "always looking on the bright side. Now let's go find Wilford and get you married, my dear."

When I thought about who would walk me down the aisle in place of my father, Wilford had immediately sprung to mind. He blushed when I asked him and said he'd be honored as he and Elaine considered me as the daughter they'd never had.

As Elaine and I walked down the hall, after making sure Ryan was already safely outside at the altar, I pondered how much my life had changed in the past two years.

Ryan and I started dating immediately after that kiss and we were so happy together. A few months later, he moved into my house. We liked nothing better than coming home at night and telling each other about our days and just spending time with each other, goofing around, and learning about each other.

True to her word, Ashley had moved to Europe with Carlos and had spent her time before that teaching me everything that I needed to know about running an event planning business. During that time, we transitioned the name of the business from Ellerbee Events to Hart to Heart Events in a play on my last name, Hartwell, and of course the main fodder of the business, which remained weddings.

Right before Ashley and Carlos moved overseas, we threw a launch party for Hart to Heart Events at the Adamson Mansion to make the transition official to the public. The place was packed and many companies as well as married couples-to-be gave me their cards, saying they were going to hire me for their events based on the detail I'd put into this party. Luckily for me and the business, each one did indeed hire Hart to Heart Events, so the company was a success.

As the party was winding down, I went from room to room to make sure all the doors were locked before we all left, and I took a moment to steal away to the library, which was still my favorite room in the house. Ryan found me there, glancing through a copy of "Little Women" that I'd found on the shelves.

"Hey, you," he said with a grin. "Not surprised at all that you're in here with a book. I was wondering where you'd gone off to."

"Oh, you know me," I replied. "Can't keep my nose out of a book and can't keep myself away from this room. Heck, it was the site of our first kiss, so how could it not be special to me?"

Putting the book back in its spot, I walked over to Ryan, wrapping my arms around his neck, pulling him to me for a kiss, knowing this time that it was indeed me kissing him instead of Dorothy kissing Walter.

After a few minutes of heady kisses, Ryan pulled away and brought me over to the couch. "I'm actually glad I found you here," Ryan said, "because I was going to bring you here anyway."

"Oh, were you now?", I grinned saucily at him. "Looking to recreate Dorothy and Walter's scene on the couch, eh? Well, sir, I'm not that kind of lady. Okay, you know otherwise, but still, Ryan, there are partygoers in the house. Let's wait til after they leave and then I'm all yours."

"You've certainly given me something to look forward to after the party," chuckled Ryan, "but that's not why I wanted to bring you here."

He stood up, and reached into his pocket, pulling out a small velvet box as he dropped to his knee in front of me, causing me to gasp.

"My dear, sweet Maura," Ryan said, "in a way our love story started here, so I thought it was the best spot for this moment. Every day that I spend with you is somehow better than the last. You have brought such love, joy, and caring into my life. Until we started dating, I didn't think love was something that was in the cards for me and that all I could settle for was companionship. But you've made me see the truth and I can only hope that I've shown you how much I love you for you -- and that entails the goofy, silly side that you spent far too long trying not to show me, and yet, that's the part of you that made me love you even more. I want to spend the rest of my life with you. So, please say you'll marry me."

"Yes!", I said, jumping off the couch and almost knocking Ryan off his feet with my hug. "I would love to be your wife, Ryan! I love you so much."

We embraced and kissed for a few minutes, until Ryan pulled back for a second. "Umm, Maura, honey. Don't you want to see the ring?," he chuckled. With that, he opened the box, showing me the simply stunning white gold engagement ring with a one karat cushion-cut diamond.

"It's beautiful," I gushed, "and it's even more gorgeous because it's from you. Yes, I will marry you, of course."

"I love you, Maura," Ryan said as he slipped the ring onto my left hand, where it fit so perfectly. "You've made me the happiest man in the world."

When we went back to the party to share our happy news, Ashley promptly declared that she'd come back and plan the event for us.

Holding our wedding at the Adamson Mansion was a no-brainer. The chandelier in the ballroom had finally been taken down and had been replaced by a number of smaller light fixtures throughout the ceiling. As for Dorothy's bedroom, where Kitty had been killed, we tossed out that mirror and armoire and replaced the flooring with antique light pink and black checked laminate flooring in her honor.

Our wedding would be the first wedding held at the Adamson Mansion since Dorothy's, but it felt right that my wedding would follow her own, and further bring light and love back into the mansion for good.

Elaine and I met Wilford, who was decked out in a snazzy black tux, at the bottom of the staircase.

"You look lovely, my dear," said Wilford as he tucked my hand into his elbow to escort me outside and into the back yard. Ashley had transformed the yard into a romantic scene complete with a white aisle runner from the house to the floral canopy, where Ryan would be waiting for me. Neither of us wanted to have any attendants as we didn't see the point, but Wilford and Elaine would be standing up with us in front of the Justice of the Peace. Our guests sat on white folding chairs with padded seats for comfort.

Ashley met us at the door that led outside next to the ballroom. She had put a white drape over the door windows so no one could see me until it was time, but I wanted to take it down as I was chomping at the bit to see everything.

She gave me a huge hug and then pushed the door opened. I gasped at the lush garden in front of me, and then my eyes went straight to Ryan to find that his eyes were locked straight on me with the most brilliant smile on his face. And then I heard "Somewhere Over the Rainbow" by Israel Kamakawiwo'ole start playing (I'd always loved that song and wanted it as my bridal entrance song) and I grinned even larger.

"Guess I don't have to drag you down the aisle," joked Wilford. "I'd say slow down, but I know that won't stop you."

Almost floating down the aisle, I shortly joined Ryan at the altar. Wilford disengaged my hand from his elbow and placed my hand in Ryan, saying "Be good to her, sir. I know you will." and then he went off to sit in the front row with Elaine as Ashley came down and sat next to Carlos in the row behind them.

"You look beautiful," said Ryan. "I have never loved you more than I do right at this very moment."

"I love you, too", I grinned back. "Let's get married." We turned and let the ceremony begin. As we were announced husband and wife after the standard "I do's", I pulled Ryan to me for a kiss and our guests exploded in applause.

Turning back up the aisle, we walked back towards the house to Hailee Stenfield's version of "I Can't Help Falling in Love with You". We'd considered having Jeff Buckley's version of "Hallelujah", which seemed fitting considering how relieved we were that we'd found each other. But then we googled the lyrics and it didn't seem all that appropriate, so we went with our other favorite song.

Next came the usual array of wedding portraits, while our guests enjoyed cocktails and appetizers in the ballroom. Soon enough, we were done with the pictures and were able to join our guests at our reception.

Sweeping into the ballroom, a quick flash of how unhappy Dorothy was entering into her reception appeared in my memory. I was so glad that Ryan and I had found true love and happiness in each other and that we were both beaming as we walked into the reception hall to WWE wrestler Daniel

Bryan's "Yes" chant entrance music, which was appropriate considering that's what I was doing when Ryan first fell for me.

We walked over to the middle of the dance floor and the DJ started playing our first dance song, which was, of course, "It Had to be You" by Frank Sinatra, thanks to "When Harry Met Sally".

As we swirled around the dance floor, I saw some shimmering objects appear. Fearing the worst, and that I may be the only one seeing them, I quickly whispered in Ryan's ear to look in the corner. He glanced over and we both smiled when we saw the ghosts of Dorothy and Walter dancing together happily to our first dance song.

"They're together now in death," I said to Ryan. "I think we made that happen and I couldn't be happier about it."

"They deserve happiness, too", said Ryan, "since in a way, they brought us together, so I'm glad they're here. And hey, some other people are here, too, to wish us well."

I looked over again and almost burst into tears when I saw Kitty and Travis' ghosts standing there, with huge grins on their faces and their arms intertwined. "I miss you," I mouthed to both of them.

They mouthed back "We love you" and both pointed next to them, and my gaze traveled past them to see the ghosts of my parents standing there, beaming with happiness.

"Are those your parents?", said Ryan. "Okay, this is amazing. Baby, you deserve this and I'm so glad they're here to wish you well. I just hope the guests can't see them."

I chuckled and glanced around at the guests. They were all watching our dance or watching our dance through their phones, or talking to each other, so thankfully no one had noticed the ghosts hanging out.

"I love you," I said silently to my parents. They nodded their heads and blew me kisses, before stepping backwards into the mist, along with Dorothy, Walter, Kitty, and Travis who all waved "bye".

"Are you okay, Maura," whispered Ryan in my ear. "That was a lot to take in right there."

"Yes, thanks for asking," I replied, "but I'm fine. Now I know that they're all fine and happy and still here and I'm so happy they were here on our wedding day. I love you so much, Mr. Alder. Thank you for being you."

"I love you, Mrs. Alder," Ryan replied. "We are going to have one hell of a blessed life together loving each other."

Spoiler alert, dear reader: We did.

The end.

ABOUT THE AUTHOR

Mary E. Hart grew up with her nose constantly in a book. She currently lives in Massachusetts with her husband and son. When she isn't writing away, editing away, or reading (or a combination of all of the above), she can be found creating and playing wrestling figure matches with her son. This is her first novel.

Mary would love to hear what you think about her book. Feel free to dash her an email at mehart@gmail.com or check out her website at www.maryehhart.com

Made in the USA
Middletown, DE
14 July 2017